Samuel French Acting Edition

Santos & Santos

by Octavio Solis

MUSIC USE NOTE

Licensees are solely responsible for obtaining formal written permission from copyright owners to use copyrighted music in the performance of this play and are strongly cautioned to do so. If no such permission is obtained by the licensee, then the licensee must use only original music that the licensee owns and controls. Licensees are solely responsible and liable for all music clearances and shall indemnify the copyright owners of the play(s) and their licensing agent, Samuel French, against any costs, expenses, losses and liabilities arising from the use of music by licensees. Please contact the appropriate music licensing authority in your territory for the rights to any incidental music.

IMPORTANT BILLING AND CREDIT REQUIREMENTS

If you have obtained performance rights to this title, please refer to your licensing agreement for important billing and credit requirements.

SANTOS & SANTOS was originally commissioned by the Eureka Theater Company. It was first produced by Thick Description in association with the Eureka Theater Company, co-presented by Theater Artaud, opening on December 10, 1993. The director was Tony Kelly, with lighting by Rick Martin, scene design by Richard Olmsted, costumes by Anna Oliver, sound design by Scott Robertson, stage management by Kristina Shute, music by David Conte, video by Raul Fernandez, Brainwave Thoughtproducts Inc., and Zapata painting by Evelyn Dykstra. The cast was as follows:

TOMAS (TOMMY)	Steven Ortiz
MIKE (MIGUEL, MICHAEL, MIKEY)	Michael Torries
FERNIE (FERNANDO, NEGRO)	Luis Saguar
VICKY (VICTORIA)	Vilma Silva
NENA (MAGDALENA)	Monica Sanchez
DON MIGUEL	Manny Fernandez
CAMACHO (C)	Kelvin Han Yee
PAMELA	Karen Amano
JUDGE BENTON	Rhonnie Washington
GONZALEZ	Jesus Mendoza
CASPER T. WILLIS	Jarion Monroe
PEGGY TOMLINSON	Blancett Reynolds
FELECIA LEE TOMLINSON	Amy Tribbey

Music was recorded at the San Francisco Conservatory of Music with the Caliente Quartete, with violin by Heide Sibley and Amy Schwartz, viola by Annie Chang, cello by Dana Glinski, bass by Jim Wilhelmson, and recording engineer Andreas Mever.

SANTOS & SANTOS received its world premiere at the Dallas Theater Center (Robert Yesselman, Managing Director) on May 2, 1995. The director was Richard Hamburger, with lighting by Chris Akerlind, scene design by Michael Yeargan, costumes by Donna M. Kress, and sound design by David Budries. The cast was as follows:

TOMAS (TOMMY)	Al Espinosa
MIKE (MIGUEL, MICHAEL, MIKEY)	Richard Chaves
FERNIE (FERNANDO, NEGRO)	Tim Perez
VICKY (VICTORIA)	Vilma Silva
NENA (MAGDALENA)	Dolores Godinez
DON MIGUEL	Everett Sifuentes
CAMACHO (C)	Adan Sanchez
PAMELA	Melissa Gallagher

CHARACTERS

TOMAS (TOMMY)	
MIKE (MIGUEL, MICHAEL, MIKEY)	The Santos Brothers
FERNIE (FERNANDO, NEGRO)	Attorneys from El Paso
VICKY (VICTORIA)	Fernie's wife
NENA (MAGDALENA)	Mike's wife
DON MIGUEL	Family patriarch, a ghost
CAMACHO (C)	Biker associate of the family
PAMELA	Secretary for Santos & Santos
JUDGE BENTON	Federal District Court Judge of San Antonio
GONZALEZ	US Attorney
CASPER T. WILLIS	Professional hitman and birder
PEGGY TOMLINSON	His wife and partner
FELECIA LEE TOMLINSON	Her daughter

SETTING

The play takes place in various cities in the Southwest, including
El Paso, Beaumont, Dallas, San Antonio, and Las Vegas.
The staging is nonrealistic.
Bracketed dialogue indicates spoken subtext.
Action is continuous.

TIME

The action takes place during the heady mid-80s.

ACT I

(A darkened room. A long, polished conference table. **TOMAS** *enters.)*

TOMAS. *Mi padre. Don Miguel Santos Carrillo.* From the town of Concordia in the State of Sinaloa, Mexico. Known for its finely crafted furniture. A craft he smuggled across hundreds of miles to El Paso. Santos Furniture Emporium.

(An old man appears, polishing the table with a rag.)

DON MIGUEL. The grain of the wood pulses toward the north.

TOMAS. His old tattoo of a heart torn at the valves glistens on his sweaty arm.

DON MIGUEL. *Mijo…*

TOMAS. Coming back. My home. In this man, all the needs of earth.

DON MIGUEL. Use only one thing, from this moment on and forever till the stars cave in and the rivers dry and the land refuses any seed. Use only this and nothing else, *mijo.*

TOMAS. *¿Que, Papa?*

DON MIGUEL. Lemon pledge.

*(**MIKE** and **FERNIE** crash through the darkness and thrust **TOMAS** on the table as **DON MIGUEL** fades.)*

MIKE. Grab his legs! Grab him!

FERNIE. I got him! Awright!

MIKE. Listen up, we're going to say this once and then life as you know it gonna change forever, understand? You never be the same!

FERNIE. Holy Holy Holy!

MIKE. You take the name of our father our blood our god in vain, you rain shit on us in the way of lies slander and insult, you turn your face against the name of Santos –

FERNIE. *(Pulling out a huge blade.)* We gut you like a pig and pull out your heart!

MIKE. Like a smoking coal, *carnal!*

FERNIE. In the name of our people, born of the whore of Cortes, *la Malinche* who betrayed her own *Raza*, this'll cut you right where you believe!

MIKE. *(As he takes out a bottle.)* This is the blood a your brothers, distilled by the gods a time!

FERNIE. Open your mouth and let family in, bro!

(The force the contents down his throat.)

MIKE. Now die motherfucker! You're not a man now, you're Santos! DIE!

FERNIE. You're dead to this world, *carnal!*

MIKE. Born again in ours! BAPTIZED IN THE BLOOD OF *LA RAZA*!

FERNIE. AAAAAAAAAAAAAAAAAAAAIIIIIIIIIIIIIIIIIIIIEEEEEEE EEEEEEEEEEE!

(They release him and break out laughing. **TOMAS** *gags.)*

TOMAS. Jesus Christ! You scared the hell out of me, man! You coulda cut me!

FERNIE. *(Showing the retractable blade.) Relajate, hombre. It's a toy knife.*

MIKE. Welcome to the firm, Tommy.

FERNIE. Check it out! Santos & Santos!

TOMAS. What was that you made me drink?

FERNIE. The worm.

MIKE. Mescal was his idea.

TOMAS. Ugghhh! I'm gonna be sick.

FERNIE. Hey, Tomas, a Santos ain't a Santos till he chomp on the worm. One of the bylaws, man, in the charter of our firm, I shit you not!

TOMAS. Damn, you *vatos* never change. You been keeping your edge.

MIKE. Just for you, bro. YOU the biggest priority in this firm.

FERNIE. That's right, *carnal,* we gonna show you the works!

TOMAS. [And they do. Papa, every inch of the premises, proud and corporate, clean and professional and dripping with efficiency]

MIKE. My office.

FERNIE. My *pinchi* office.

MIKE. Yours over here.

FERNIE. Conference room.

MIKE. John.

FERNIE. Copier, toner on that shelf.

MIKE. Fax machine.

(PAMELA enters, file in hand.)

PAM. Sign, Mike.

FERNIE. *Orale!* Pam! Tomas, this is the lady I was telling you about.

TOMAS. Hi, my name's Tommy. I'm the new blood here.

PAM. Don't go spilling it on me, junior.

FERNIE. Listen up. Pamela types eighty words a minute, knows Wordperfect 6-1, does filework something fierce. Great voice on the phone, great public manner, great fucking legs. She's really good.

PAM. Your brother's a slime.

TOMAS. I know.

FERNIE. She used to work the tables in Vegas. Card shooter from the Sands.

TOMAS. So why'd you wanna come work for these losers?

PAM. I needed to get away from that shit for awhile.

FERNIE. She's a pro, Tommy. You'll like her.

TOMAS. Those eighty words a minute are gonna double once I get started. Time and a half gonna be your middle name.

PAM. I think it's time we talked raise, Mike.

> (**PAM** *goes.*)

FERNIE. I'm gonna bone that babe!

MIKE. Let's hit the road!

TOMAS. Is this your Lexus?

FERNIE. Hop in!

TOMAS. [And to the town of my birth, the sun city, pass of the north.]

MIKE. Your pueblo, bro!

FERNIE. *El Chuco!*

TOMAS. Things haven't changed a bit!

MIKE. These are your people!

FERNIE. Your lowrider babes!

TOMAS. Man, I been missing this bad!

MIKE. They been missin' you!

TOMAS. HEY! HAVE YOU BEEN INJURED AT WORK OR IN AN AUTO ACCIDENT? WERE YOU HURT IN AN ON-THE-JOB MISHAP? YOU'RE ENTITLED TO COMPENSATION! NO RECOVERY NO FEE! CALL NOW!

FERNIE. GOOD CREDIT, BAD CREDIT, NO CREDIT! *¡SE HABLA ESPAÑOL!*

MIKE. Gird your loins for the Big Time!

TOMAS. El Paso County Courthouse!

FERNIE. Now we do business!

TOMAS. Let's boogie.

> (**MIKE** *and* **FERNIE** *split off to separate areas.*)

MIKE. On behalf of my client I am requesting that the charges be reduced to a single charge of fiduciary irresponsibility considering the reparations which my client has already initiated to the plaintiff.

FERNIE. As these diagrams indicate, the bullet's point of entry was in the upper abdomen, but the exit wound was above the left nipple which deems it impossible for my client to have fired the alleged shots.

TOMAS. [*Santos y Santos. Los Carnales de* Criminal Defense. Hustling for the raza, taking a stand for the community.]

MIKE. At what time was this warrant obtained? Did you not present this warrant six hours after the search and seizure of Mr. Saucedo's property? Did the magistrate know the search was being illegally conducted?

FERNIE. These depositions contradict the witness' prior testimony, which not only proves that the City Attorney is not above using perjured testimony but also clears Señor. Garza of any wrongdoing in the case.

TOMAS. [This was it. The vision that drew me back. No more Thomas B. Santos esq., the prodigal son in San Diego, at the District Attorney's desk, prosecuting my race according to an alien penal code. Now it was Tomas Santos, the People's Defender, the new blood.]

MIKE/FERNIE. We believe our clients are guilty of no crime but the crime of Mexican descent, and that, your honor, ain't no crime at all.

TOMAS. God, I love watching you guys in action.

MIKE. I gotta meeting.

(*He goes.*)

FERNIE. Here. Potential clients. Meet Pam at the Law Library. Eleven sharp.

(FERNIE goes as PAM enters.)

PAM. Glad you could make it. You look up those cases, I'll take these. Hurry, you gotta be back at the court by one for Mike's wife.

TOMAS. Nena?

(PAM goes as NENA enters.)

NENA. Hey, pretty boy! Good to see your ass! Everyone was asking about you at Papa Santos' funeral. *Toma,* my man forgot these depos in the *pinchi* day care. Make sure he gets them.

TOMAS. You look fabulous!

NENA. I know.

(NENA goes as FERNIE and MIKE return.)

MIKE. Two o'clock. We gotta date, fellas. In the car.

TOMAS. [And drive, past the same storefronts, the same car lots, the same squalor, to El Paso Evergreen Cemetery.]

(They halt. TOMAS slowly comes to his knees as his brothers regard him.)

[Santo, santo, santo, *padre todopodrido,* dead, buried, boxed in Concordia wood, put to rest on American soil, next to my mother, two slabs who begot me, two slabs inscribed with names, dates, recriminations. How do you ask the dead for peace?]

FERNIE. Mike, let's call it a day and head back to the office.

MIKE. We're there, bro.

(They are. Conference table.)

TOMAS. I felt him, Mike. I asked him to forgive me all my sins against my people, and I felt his mercy. This is what the courts are missing. That's why none of us really believes we can get a fair trial. But if we could just apply the truth of the people to the people, then, *vatos,* we got it made!

MIKE. Oh fuck. Are you talking about doing *pro bono* work?

(CAMACHO comes in, carrying a gym bag.)

CAMACHO. Yo. Mike.

MIKE. Come on in, C. Tomas, you remember Camacho, don't you?

TOMAS. Camacho. I thought you were dead.

CAMACHO. Hey.

FERNIE. C helps us with deliveries, courier shit. He bends over backwards, this guy.

CAMACHO. Naw.

FERNIE. He does. The only one left from the old days. Brass knuckles and pop guns, right, ese?

CAMACHO. Damn.

TOMAS. Are you still a man of few words, C?

CAMACHO. Naw.

MIKE. *Oye,* we just got the news. *Este chingon* is joining our firm.

CAMACHO. Great. Party.

TOMAS. What you got in the gym bag, C?

CAMACHO. In here?

FERNIE. In there?

TOMAS. What's in the bag, C?

CAMACHO. Nothin'.

FERNIE. *Nada,* bro.

TOMAS. I asked you to quit this shit for me. You told me you would.

FERNIE. It's not that easy, Tommy.

TOMAS. I locked up and extradited to Mexico hundreds of men, some of them hardly men at all, for dealing in this kinda shit. It sickens me. I can't deal with it anymore.

MIKE. Okay. C, open it.

> (**CAMACHO** *places the gym bag on the table, gingerly unwrapping a small bundle.*)

CAMACHO. Sweet bread.
Mrs. Herrera. She got a boy, only sixteen. Busted for drunk driving. Gave the cop attitude. Was gonna go

from juvie to jail. Only Mike and Fernie cut a deal, sent him home sober. Old lady got no money, but she makes her own bread.

TOMAS. Okay. So I was wrong. Sorry, C.

MIKE. This is your homecoming, Tommy. We don't want to mess it up.

FERNIE. What's the deal anyway? A little coke, a little weed, among friends, this is America, for crying out loud.

TOMAS. [That's right, Papa. Crying out loud. America crying out loud in my head, bouncing off the prison walls, *se habla español, se habla tattoo,* at the top of their lungs, crying for vindication, they want something pure, just, good, sweet, like sweet bread, the Modern Mexican is not a Mexican at all, he's an American, for crying out loud.]

(**PAM** *comes in with the same painting as before.*)

PAM. Here you go, new boy.

TOMAS. What's this?

FERNIE. Your present! Straight from Vegas! Flight babe almost broke it on the way. *Ten, carnal,* with all our bitchen love.

MIKE. May you win many judgments.

(*A velvet painting of Zapata on his white horse.*)

TOMAS. Nice. I guess.

FERNIE. It's supposed to be Zapata, man, but don't you think he looks more like me?

TOMAS. He sure don't look like Zapata.

FERNIE. *Calmantes montes, bro.* You're missing the horse, ese. Zapata's famous horse.

(**FERNIE** *smears a wet finger on the horse. Tastes it.*)

Party.

TOMAS. Cocaine?

PAM. No, baking soda.

CAMACHO. Cool.

FERNIE. This artist pal in Taos ships it round the world like this! He used to get high with Dennis Hopper. Ride this pony, *cabrones!*

TOMAS. I thought you said –

FERNIE. It's just a gag gift, *ese! ¡Andale! Nomas una linea.*

MIKE. We gotta be straight for the LULAC presentation, Negro.

FERNIE. You are such pussies!

MIKE. Pam. Go through the book and find a shop that'll fit this man with an Armani by seven o'clock this evening.

PAM. Right away.

(She goes.)

FERNIE. Ouch! You see the ass on that babe? Aww, I'm gonna bone her, you watch! She's been fighting me off too long. Time I boned her.

MIKE. Case you haven't heard, Fernie fucks all the secretaries.

TOMAS. What does Vicky think of this?

FERNIE. You watch. I'll bone her, I swear to you, the chick is mine!

CAMACHO. Cut it out, Fernie. *Pasiguate.*

FERNIE. Hey, C, you just keep an eye on Vicky and everything'll be cool.

MIKE. Enough of this. Party's waitin'.

TOMAS. Mike, I have to tell you guys about this idea –

FERNIE. Just a fucking minute! We got Toltec cocaina here bearing the seal of the Santos Family for our new partner. Is this gesture going to be ignored and thereby dissed?

MIKE. Tomas?

TOMAS. *(Slowly approaching the line.)* [A thin white scar on the table, my father's table, his memory, the sentence of all my suspects, powdered like sweet bread, symbols in search of symbols on the fine grain of the wood facing north, where all good things are, the best homes, the best clothes, the best laws, the best jails, the best kind of death, plunging downward, downward, falling toward heaven, oh what the hell, just once, just for them, my brothers, my family, *mi raza.*]

> (**TOMAS** *snorts up the line.*)

Let's go buy me a Lexus!

FERNIE. Damn straight!

CAMACHO. Fuckin' A!

MIKE. You are blood!

> *(They begin undressing him as* **PAM** *comes on carrying a new suit. As they dress* **TOMAS**, **JUDGE** **BENTON** *enters, orating at the banquet.)*

JUDGE. These boys, these boys, these incorrigible boys. Proud first generation American scions of an immigrant cabinet maker, an importer of furniture, the brothers of the Law Firm of Santos & Santos blah blah blah blah blah

blah

blah blood stewing on my tongue for lying for Miguel and Fernando stinkos, two of the most

invidious,

corrupt,

treacherous,

racketeering

by god the finest attorneys in this state's legal fandangos. In a few short years they have made their firm among the most honored blah blah

blah

blah

blasphemy that's what this is but for politics' sake the show must go on but whoa whoa doggie, this boy, this new one, I know from San Diego, good son, good skin, good eyes, indeed a santo to behold, but my tribute diarrhears its ugly head again

again

again I say these turks have won many admirable and deserving judgments at the highest level of the Texas court, and even in my docket, they have a spectacular reputation for success blah

blah

blah

black eyes black hair this Tomas has a whoreson look to him, abandonment, a look which judges me, by what right, no right, I'm a good man, I love my wife and daughter, I stand by the immutable laws of this land, I'm a populist, I voted for LBJ, I'm an intellectual, I voted for Nixon, but this young man has a mission but

but

but it's in the community that they have distinguished themselves, providing scholarships to high school students blah blah blah

blah

blandly how he looks at me, like all Mexicans look, with dull opaque eyes into my heart, where a fear is beshat and a deep anathema, sing the national anathema, jose can you see, from the halls of Montezuma, we will fight and be free

free

free free law clinics at the community college, substantial in-kind services to needy groups blah

blah

blah

set an example for all people in the Sun City blah blah blah blah

blah

latino constituents blah blah blah

blast this golden litigator who cannot transcend the political reality which is to suck up to this mob for the cameras which is to testify on behalf of these scalawags which is to sit upon my bench till the president appoints me to the supremes, where I will shimmy to the constitution shakedown, political reality is neither political nor real, but this Santos runt, this beautiful boy, he pierces my soul with a message deep dark and bla-

blah

blah

blah

My great privilege to present this plaque to Miguel and Fernando Santos, Attorneys at Law, on behalf of the El Paso LULAC Council. For exemplary service to the community.

> *(Applause.* **MIKE** *and* **FERNIE** *receive the plaque.* **TOMAS**, *now in his suit, watches with interest.)*

MIKE. Thank you, sir. I count that tribute our greatest victory.

FERNIE. Hustle, Mike. Chimichanga's getting cold.

MIKE. Let me announce that our law firm is presenting a charitable contribution to the LULAC Council in the amount of $20,000.

> *(Applause.* **MIKE** *gives the check to the* **JUDGE**, *who receives it with a smile.)*

JUDGE. Then by God, LET'S EAT.

> *(Music. Lights change. On another area,* **TOMAS** *stands in the parking lot.* **FERNIE** *dashes over to him.)*

FERNIE. *Que paso, bro.* My wife here yet?

TOMAS. I've seen three Beemers, none hers. Where's Nena?

FERNIE. Bathroom. She's not feeling good. *Alomejor* es un *pinchi* flu.

TOMAS. Negro, what the hell is Benton doing here? You guys are supposed to be mortal enemies.

FERNIE. Times are changing, bro. The word is this overfed country club judge is heading for the Big Court.

TOMAS. No way. Benton? Supreme Court? He's too far to the right for it.

FERNIE. Not anymore. He's sending his valentines to all minority PACs in the state. He wants to shine in the Congressional Record. What the fuck, it's putting us in the Bar Journal. Yo, here they come. Listen. Tomorrow we're all going to Vegas to celebrate your recruitment, and I'm gonna bring Pam along. If Vicky asks, we're just us three going, okay?

(**CAMACHO** *and* **VICKY** *enter.*)

Hey, buttheads, you're too late. It's over. Food's cold.

CAMACHO. Sorry, Fern.

FERNIE. No problem, it's only a dinner in my fucking honor.

VICKY. Don't yell at me, Negro. It's been a bad day.

FERNIE. Whoa. Pardon me, princess. What's the excuse this time?

VICKY. I was on the phone.

FERNIE. Who with, one of your boyfriends?

VICKY. No, one of your girlfriends, Fernando. She called because she wants to know how serious we are about each other.

FERNIE. You're out of your mind.

VICKY. I told her we made vows before God and the priest and everybody, but they're negotiable. Everything's negotiable, baby.

CAMACHO. Sorry, Fernie.

FERNIE. I can't believe you listen to those *pendejas*. You poison yourself with their shit.

VICKY. Makes you think, though, don't it?

FERNIE. Great attitude. Great. Here. Say hello to my brother.

TOMAS. How you doing, Vicky?

VICKY. Tommy. How was your flight down?

TOMAS. A little bumpy. You still in charge of the furniture store?

VICKY. My ball and chain. Sorry I'm all…

TOMAS. I understand.

CAMACHO. Sorry, Fernie.

FERNIE. *(As NENA enters, looking a bit queasy.)* Will you quit saying you're sorry, goddammit. This is a happy occasion. Here comes Nena! NENA! Hey, *cuñada,* nauseous from the nachos?

NENA. *¡Oye, oye, oye! Mira este.* I'm fine. Something in the food just took a detour.

FERNIE. They don't put enough *chile* in it. Bland motherfucking shit.

CAMACHO. Hi, Nena.

NENA. Macho Camacho. Glad you made it, Vicky. We wondered about you.

VICKY. I don't like schmoozing. Looks like I missed it, anyway.

NENA. *Pero ahora sigue el pisto.* You get to drink with those old *pelados* who look down your blouse. Take my advice, just smile, nod, ask them about their wives every now and then *y diles* to vote Democrat. *Ven con nosotros adentro.*

FERNIE. Hey, before I forget, ladies, we're off to Las Vegas tomorrow morning, Mike bought the tickets, we gonna hang for a couple.

NENA. *¿Otra vez?*

TOMAS. I just found out myself.

VICKY. Can I come?

FERNIE. He only got three tickets. It's a brother thing. We're gonna show this guy a good time. C here'll take care of you.

VICKY. Yeah. The sprayhead.

FERNIE. Hey! Watch your mouth –

TOMAS. YA! *(Silence.)* You know where our father comes from? Concordia. Concord. Agreement. Getting along, let's get along, let's have some beer and let's agree.

NENA. Let 'em go, Vicky. It'll be good to get the testosterone out of the house. *Nomas dile a Miguel* to bring back something nice for the girls. Some dolls and shit.

FERNIE. C'mon. *(To* VICKY.*)* You learn some respect.

(NENA *and* FERNIE *go.)*

CAMACHO. You want me to bring you a plate?

VICKY. No, listen, why don't you go and help yourself? I'm not so hungry. Go on.

(CAMACHO *goes.* VICKY *opens her purse and produces a vial. She sniffs a tiny spoonful.)*

Fucking Negro. Like I don't know what he's up to. Like I'm some idiot. You want a hit?

TOMAS. I'll pass.

VICKY. Who's he taking with him?

TOMAS. Nobody.

VICKY. Fine, don't tell me. God forbid I should make you rat on your brothers. I got my ways of dealing with him.

TOMAS. Are you going to stay out here?

(VICKY *nods and turns away.)*

VICKY. [Linger –

TOMAS. We linger –

VICKY. Longing –

TOMAS. To want her back –

VICKY. My back to him I feel –

TOMAS. I feel I hurt I misgive –

VICKY. Misgive the memory gone so cold.]

TOMAS. Vicky, about the past –

VICKY. I got no past. All I got is Santos Furniture Emporium and *(showing him the vial)* this.

TOMAS. You don't remember us?

<table>
<tr><td>

VICKY.
[No recall no goodbye something kissed something bland halfhearted something halfsaid an older brother's comfort his fire his ring his wife.]

</td><td>

TOMAS.
[Purely her even now.]

</td></tr>
</table>

VICKY. Why'd you come back, Tommy? Now, out of the clear blue…

TOMAS. I couldn't bear San Diego. The cases I kept getting. Luna, Franco, Ramirez, Pedrazo, they just kept coming at me like flyweight boxers. Swollen Indian faces fulla guilt.

VICKY. [We're all guilty, *concordia* to *discordia,* our faces, riven wide, eyes full of whatever happens happens.]

(*The* **JUDGE** *enters and watches, unseen by them.*)

TOMAS. The day Dad passed away, I was cross-examining an old guy, an illegal. He was crying because his son had died in a chase for both of them at the border. They'd come across at night and when *La Migra* chased them, the son ran off a cliff, all the way down, plunging like the peso, to the land of his salvation. The old guy blamed himself… I couldn't help thinking of Papa, dying without me at his side.

VICKY. Well, he's gone and you're here. What do you think you can accomplish now?

TOMAS. Something inside, Vicky, there's a seed of something…right.

VICKY. What is it?

TOMAS. It's wild. I can't even say.

JUDGE. Try.

TOMAS. Who's there?

(*He comes forward.*)

JUDGE. Try to say.

VICKY. Let's go inside, Tommy.

JUDGE. I'd like to have a word with you, son.

VICKY. We're not interested.

JUDGE. Please stay.

TOMAS. Go on, Vicky. Save me a plate.

> (VICKY *goes.* TOMAS *and the* JUDGE *regard each other.*)

JUDGE. I am William Louis Benton.

TOMAS. I know who you are, sir. Why aren't you inside eating?

JUDGE. I don't like Mexican. It corrupts my digestion. Tomas Santos, you have something to tell me.

TOMAS. Do I?

JUDGE. I felt the cataclysm in you, during my speech. Tell it to me, son.

TOMAS. Nothing to tell.

> (*The* JUDGE *turns his gaze out toward the horizon.*)

JUDGE. That's Ciudad Juarez over there, isn't it? That country puts the fear of God in me. They have a whole different concept of the Law. I went there once, to La Mariscal. A dingy little street lined up with painted prostitutes.

TOMAS. I know it.

JUDGE. I met the only whore I ever knew that night. Paloma. A pretty young thing, blessed with what I call the eyes of mercy. I saw her on several occasions until one day I looked into her and I saw a fire burst through her eyes. She told me we were conceiving my child. A boy. That's when I stopped going to La Mariscal.

TOMAS. What's that got to do with me?

JUDGE. Nothing, maybe. But you and me are of one heart. I know your terror. Your vision.

TOMAS. You do?

JUDGE. I've felt it, like in Paloma. Tell me your cataclysm.

TOMAS. I'm not sure...

JUDGE. I believe in you.

TOMAS. Don't get me wrong. I love my people.

JUDGE. By God, I love them too –

TOMAS. It is not our fault –

JUDGE. No way –

TOMAS. It's a cycle. We've bred ourselves to live –

JUDGE. Vicious cycle –

TOMAS. American cycle: birth, arrest, arraignment, hearing, conviction, death –

JUDGE. Lubricated by tears and pace picante sauce –

TOMAS. The bill of rights stays on the right –

JUDGE. And the constitution ain't bilingual –

TOMAS. We're bastards of the Law, your honor, illegitimate three-headed freaks of nature –

JUDGE. Jails and jokes are full of you –

TOMAS. But on his arm, my father had a tattoo emblazoned like a sign –

JUDGE. That's right, boy, a sign –

TOMAS. That's what we need, a sign, a symbol, we respond to symbols, they invigorate us, they purge and guide us, they give us hope and meaning –

JUDGE. This country was built on abstractions, on concepts you and me can't see, touch, taste, fuck, or light candles to –

TOMAS. We need a symbol for justice, not this nameless lady with the blind and scales –

JUDGE. Impeach her, by god –

TOMAS. Give her a name, paint her in bright red and green, give her terra cotta skin, and put a brilliant corona around her –

JUDGE. A whole six-pack of coronas –

TOMAS. Tear the blind off so we can see her gleaming eyes –

JUDGE. One blue one brown and make the book she holds a bowl of cornmeal –

TOMAS. Because corn is universal and you can't eat a fucking book –

JUDGE. A new vision of justice –

TOMAS. *LA VIRGEN DE JUSTICIA* –

JUDGE. Appointed by the people for a drug-free America –

TOMAS. *Our sierra madre oriental* –

JUDGE. Lactating blood for the masses –

TOMAS. *La leche de* human blindness –

JUDGE. Boundless to all races –

TOMAS. *ROPA PARA TODA LA FAMILIA* –

JUDGE. MOLE WITH YOUR METHADONE –

TOMAS. DUTY-FREE GOODS –

JUDGE. FREE-TRADE AGREEMENTS –

TOMAS. AND ALL THE REHAB PROGRAMS, THE CITIZEN PATROLS, THE INTERDICTION AND STIFF SENTENCING, THE DEATH PENALTIES WILL BE OBSOLETE –

JUDGE. DRUG-TURF CRIME WILL VANISH ACROSS THE COUNTRY –

TOMAS. AND THE RACE OF MONTEZUMA WILL AT LAST ACHIEVE FULL CITIZENSHIP –

JUDGE. YES YES YESSSSSS!

TOMAS. DON'T GET ME WRONG I LOVE MY PEOPLE

JUDGE. IT SHOWS IN EVERY FIBER OF YOUR BEING –

> *(Pause. They catch their breath.)*

Come work for me.

TOMAS. I'm with Santos & Santos.

JUDGE. You can't mean what you say and still be with your brothers. Not the way they live.

TOMAS. My brothers are good.

JUDGE. You're the only good son, Tomas. Those two are working cheek-by-jowl with known traffickers, horse-tradin' them back to the streets where they can spread their gospel. You want your symbol defiled like that?

> *(He starts to leave.)*

Paloma is my symbol. And you, boy, you have her eyes.

(He goes.)

TOMAS. [He knows my cataclysm, Papa.]

> *(Inside the firm.* **PAM** *enters with a sheaf of papers.)*

PAM. These are for your Federal Income taxes, these are Bar membership, and these are for your health insurance. Press down hard. There are four copies.

> *(***TOMAS*** *takes them.* **MIKE** *and* **FERNIE***, already dressed for Vegas, ferret through the documents.)*

Sign these depositions, Mike. They're proofed, copied, and ready to go.

MIKE. Thanks, Pam.

PAM. You got a call from the Natural Gas Company re that pipeline agreement. And Mrs. Herrera is sending over some more bread. Fernando, the DA's been calling for you all morning.

FERNIE. Oh, yeah. Frank. We had a golf date.

PAM. The Vegas tickets. You're on American 662 at 2:35. First class.

FERNIE. Hey, Pamela, you wanna come with?

PAM. Sorry. Got loads to do here.

MIKE. Did you have a good time last night, *carnal?*

TOMAS. Great.

FERNIE. What a blowout, man. Really took off once we lost those fat city council fucks. *(Laughs.)*

PAM. Was that the mayor who kept coming on to me?

MIKE. He was drunk out of his skull. Tommy, Vicky said you and Benton had a talk last night.

TOMAS. We shot the shit.

MIKE. What did you have to say to each other?

TOMAS. Academic stuff, mainly. The guy was required reading at Stanford.

> *(***CAMACHO*** *enters with the gym bag.)*

MIKE. Watch yourself around him. He doesn't appreciate the work we do.

FERNIE. He's a fucking racist!

MIKE. Before his immaculate conversion, he was for tightening up the border between here and Baja Tejas. He wanted radar balloons and armed surveillance of the *rio*.

CAMACHO. *¿El juez?*

MIKE. Yeah. Got the bread?

CAMACHO. Right here.

MIKE. Then let's go roll the bones.

 (They start to go.)

TOMAS. *Hermanos. (They stop.)* I want us to be honest with each other.

FERNIE. What are you talking about?

TOMAS. Are we still dealing? If we are, I wanna know.

FERNIE. Negro, shut the fuck up. C?

 *(**CAMACHO** opens the gym bag and carefully extracts a stack of bills and a small bag of coke.)*

CAMACHO. Sweet bread.

FERNIE. Mother of God!

CAMACHO. Plane landed last night. Presidio. Totally legit. Stashed in the horse trailer for pick-up tomorrow.

MIKE. And the bread?

CAMACHO. Very fresh.

FERNIE. Fuckin' A!

PAM. Winner's circle, boys. Two and a half mil.

FERNIE. Six hundred pounds. Wall to wall unprocessed Colombian purity!

MIKE. You see, Tomas, these wops from Vegas want some shit but they think they're too good to mess with the cartels and vice versa. –

PAM. They're all cut from the same cloth –

MIKE. So we negotiate the deal from them. The Colombians ship the goods, the wise guys bring the cash, and no one has to face no-one but us. We make the link-up.

FERNIE. Shit, we're the only ones fluent in both languages.

TOMAS. I don't get it. How in the world did we get mixed up in this shit? You guys are icons. You don't need this.

MIKE. This is how the world works, brother. It's what we do for the good of our bloods and our business. Sure it sucks, but it makes our charity work fly, it's enabled the education of our brothers and sisters, and reinforced our image as positive role models.

FERNIE. We can rise on this crop, *ese,* if the profits are used right. Imagine what harm this could do in the hands of real criminals.

PAM. Most of it gets intercepted by the DEA down the pipeline, anyway.

MIKE. Tomas, this has given us power. Power to help our community. To give them the kind of justice they deserve.

CAMACHO. Sweet bread, Tomas.

FERNIE. Fuck this! C'mon, celebrate! Pam, you and me, Vegas!

PAM. You never give up, do you?

FERNIE. I got a big suite reserved with a round bed.

PAM. Take no for an answer, Fernie.

FERNIE. I'm your type, girl. *Puro indio.* I be yo' bullfighter.

PAM. You might not believe this, but I got better things to do than hang with you in a city I have no heart for.

FERNIE. What's the matter? Don't you like boys?

PAM. As a matter of fact, no. I don't. Have a nice trip.

(*She goes.* **MIKE** *and* **CAMACHO** *laugh.*)

FERNIE. Did you hear that? Oh my god! I got a dyke working here! I brought an actual dyke!

CAMACHO. Serves your ass right, Fernie.

MIKE. Sign those papers, Tommy, and let's move.

FERNIE. I don't believe it! She's got a body like that and she's a lesbian! This is terrible! Fire her ass, Mikey!

MIKE. Uh-uh. She stays.

FERNIE. But she's a lesbian, man. You heard her!

MIKE. I'm not losing the only top-shelf secretary we ever had.

CAMACHO. I think that shit's illegal anyway.

FERNIE. All right, keep her. But I say I'm still gonna bone her first chance she gives me. Dyke or no dyke.

MIKE. That's another thing. You are not harassing her while she sits behind that desk. I don't give a shit how hard up you are, you don't say anything, do anything, whatever, that will jeopardize her position in this firm. You try your shit on her, and I'll go to Vicky.

FERNIE. Just a goddamn minute! –

MIKE. I'm not finished, Fernando. Now, I don't like to butt in on your personal life, it's your business and I respect that, but this fucking shit that you're pulling is driving everyone crazy. It's affecting the family and that's no good, man. Go bone whoever you want and hurt your wife in the heart, fine, but keep your paws off my secretary. *¿Me entiendes?*

FERNIE. My wife is my business.

MIKE. And Pamela is my business. *Dejala en paz.* Tommy, mark off Monday next week. You're meeting with the legal staff at EP Savings.

(He passes some documents to **FERNIE.***)*

Here, give these to Pam to send off. They were due yesterday.

FERNIE. Fuck her.

MIKE. What's your problem, Fernie? This is an attitude I detect, then you better let me know. I won't put up with your bullshit.

TOMAS. [Bullshit, pounding in my head, buy into, baby, live in the real, know what is known, deal with, Papa, this table, this firm, this town all boned bought and paid for.]

*(***PAM** *enters.)*

PAM. Mike, wives are here.

NENA. Okay, *babosos*, this is a raid! The chicks are here to bust up your boy's club.

VICKY. *¡Mira nomas!* Suitcases! Plane tickets!

NENA. *Oye*, no-one leaves this pueblo without the *viejas'* permission!

VICKY. Think we're gonna let you guys leave without sayin' goodbye?

NENA. Fuck that shit. It's the money I want. *Orale*, gimme that skin. *¡La cartera!*

MIKE. *(Handing over his wallet.)* We weren't going to forget you ladies.

VICKY. *(To* **FERNIE.***)* What are you so quiet about?

NENA. Honey, is this all you have in here? Get with the program. It's White Flower Day at Macy's, man!

> *(***FERNIE*** kisses* **VICKY** *fiercely.)*

VICKY. Damn, Negro.

FERNIE. I love my wife. I don't give a shit. I love my wife.

VICKY. *(Kissing him back.)* I love you too, babe.

NENA. *¿Que paso?* Did Fernie lose the house playing poker?

MIKE. Nah. It's a long story. Leave it.

NENA. *¿Y porque tiene la cara larga este guey?*

MIKE. He's bummed about our sweet bread.

NENA. *¡Chale*, Tomas! This ain't no pussy California. This is El Chuco. Here *en El Paso*, you get by any way you can. Even when you got *the pinchi* morning sickness.

MIKE. What?

NENA. You might as well know, *Viejo*, I'm pregnant.

FERNIE. *¡Puta madre!*

TOMAS. A baby?

VICKY. That's great!

MIKE. How far?

NENA. Six weeks.

> *(He approaches her and sinks to his knees before her.)*

MIKE. Six weeks. *Hijo mano.* Little brown shitkicker must be at least the size of my thumbnail by now.

PAM. Maybe this time it'll be a boy, Mike.

FERNIE. We'll be laying odds on that in Vegas.

NENA. *Ten cuidado…porque sabes muy bien que te adoro.*

MIKE. Administrative fiat. You are coming to Vegas.

NENA. I can't. Who's going to take care of the girls?

VICKY. I don't mind watching them, Nena.

TOMAS. And you might as well use my ticket.

FERNIE. No way!

TOMAS. C'mon. She's going to have a baby. Besides, man, you're gonna be late for the plane. Here. *Mi regalo para ti, cuñada.*

NENA. I didn't mean to bitch on you like that. You're good.

MIKE. Brother, you make us shine.

NENA. *¡Pues a Las Fuckin' Vegas!*

> *(She rushes out with **MIKE**, **FERNIE**, and **PAM** amid a chorus of congratulations.)*

VICKY. *(To **TOMAS**.)* It looks like it's just you and me.

CAMACHO. An' me.

VICKY. Yeah.

> *(**VICKY** goes. **CAMACHO** starts after her.)*

TOMAS. C.

CAMACHO. Yo.

TOMAS. You sure the trailer's secure at…

CAMACHO. Gila Stables. Yeah, tight as a bud.

> *(As **CAMACHO** goes, the **JUDGE** in his robes strolls on.)*

JUDGE. [Cataclysms, boy. Catechisms.

TOMAS. *La sangre crying crying* legal or loyal, swelling in my head the old man crying for his son falling over falling into America –

JUDGE. Our symbol for a browner justice pimped on La Mariscal the law shoved up her constitution.

TOMAS. Burning, my fucking race burning me, your honor, I'm burning –

JUDGE. Hot plate! Hot plate! No touch! No touch!

TOMAS. I feel the breach in me –

JUDGE. The pang of your convictions, twenty to life, thirty to life, life everlasting.

TOMAS. *No puedo no puedo.*

JUDGE. You're the good son sanctify the sign stop the bleeding make it real pick up the phone –

TOMAS. Don't get me wrong I love my people –

JUDGE. Sure you do.]

> *(***TOMAS*** picks up the phone. ***FERNIE****'s anguished cry from offstage. Crossfade to the casino. ***FERNIE*** charges in, his cry leading him in.)*

FERNIE. *(Rolling a pair of dice.)* YYYYYYAAAHHHHHHH! Awright awright awright! How much! Okay! Go double! Right there! Put it there! Here we go!

> *(***MIKE*** comes in with ***NENA*** on his arm.)*

MIKE. C'mon, Fernie. That table don't like you.

FERNIE. You kidding? It loves me! It wants to suck my dick! I'm making some money here!

NENA. You better be. *Esos son mis* chips you're betting with, Negro.

FERNIE. I dedicate this holy roll to the fortunes of the next Santos kid! May he be a son and may he wear steel-toe boots! *(He rolls.)*

MIKE. Snake-eyes!

FERNIE. FUCK!

NENA. I know! *Vamonos al* jacuzzi and let's order martinis.

FERNIE. No jacuzzi. I don't want her barfin' in there. One more.

  *(**PEGGY** enters.)*

PEGGY. Michael!

MIKE. Peggy, how's it going? Haven't seen you in a coon's age.

FERNIE. Yo, Peg.

PEGGY. Furnace, how you doin', boy

NENA. You know this woman?

MIKE. Hell, we've known Peg for years!

PEGGY. He was my lawyer. You got me a suspended sentence on that weapons charge!

MIKE. Peg, this is my wife. Magdalena.

PEGGY. *Mucho gusto. ¿Como esta?*

NENA. Fine. How the hell are you?

PEGGY. Well, guess what, Mike, I'm married now! Willis is my new name, and we're spending our honeymoon in our old stompin' ground and now all of a sudden BOOM here ya're too!

MIKE. You're a sight!

FERNIE. Yeah, you look great, babe!

NENA. *Vamos, Miguel.*

  *(**WILLIS** and **FELECIA** enter.)*

WILLIS. Darlin'.

PEGGY. Oh! Lemme introduce my husband and my girl. This is Casper.

WILLIS. Casper T. Willis. Howdy.

  *(**WILLIS** frisks **MIKE**. Tears the buttons from his cuff.)*

PEGGY. He don't like his voice on tape.

MIKE. Miguel Santos.

PEGGY. And this is the flower of my life, Felecia Lee.

FELECIA. Y'all got any pot?

PEGGY. Keep a civil tongue in your head, young lady. You don't know who these people are.

FERNIE. Watch it, little girl. We're lawyers.

MIKE. What's with the buttons?

WILLIS. If truth be told, Mr. Santos, I've just come out of Leavenworth.

FERNIE. Maximum security. What were you in for?

WILLIS. Thisnthat. Braggin', mainly.

PEGGY. A wire took years off my baby's life, but he is still a experienced handler of people.

FELECIA. Who looks older, me or her?

PEGGY. Shush, you.

NENA. I want to go to the jacuzzi, Miguel.

WILLIS. I'm not cheap, sir, but I'm reliable.

PEGGY. And convenient! We live in Texas, too! Beaumont! You know what they say, if you can scratch your balls, you can make the calls...to Beaumont! *(Laughs.)*

NENA. Miguel...

MIKE. Mr. Willis. Pleasure meeting you.

WILLIS. Anytime. My card.

> **(WILLIS** *gives his card and the buttons as they leave.)*

NENA. *¿Quien es esa mujer? ¿De donde la conoces?*

MIKE. Why, you don't like her?

FERNIE. Peg's cool. She was a parole officer till she started falling for her cons. Her old man, though, you see his eyes? Like a set of bullet holes.

NENA. *Andale, quiero ponerme ese* swimsuit while it still fits.

FERNIE. Be right up. I'll get the martinis.

> **(MIKE** *and* **NENA** *leave.* **FERNIE** *produces another stack of chips.* **FELECIA** *appears.)*

FELECIA. So do you?

FERNIE. Do I what?

FELECIA. You know. Pot.

FERNIE. Yeah. I got some. Up in my room.

FELECIA. I can't go to your room.

FERNIE. Oh, I didn't know you were a minor.

FELECIA. I'm older than I look. I'm almost eighteen.

FERNIE. Then what are we waiting for?

FELECIA. I don't know you that well yet.

FERNIE. My friends call me Fernie. Some people call me Negro but I'll cut anyone outside the family who calls me that.

FELECIA. My name begins with an F too.

FERNIE. Felicia Lee Willis.

FELECIA. Tomlinson. Casper's just my stepdaddy.

FERNIE. He's big guy, huh?

FELECIA. Oh, he's terrific. He's like what, you know, when you think of the Texas Rangers, you think of him. Big. Bold. Frontier.

FERNIE. Uh-huh. Big badass motherfucking white sheriff-type of asshole.

FELECIA. That's not very nice.

FERNIE. Neither is your father.

FELECIA. What floor you on?

(**WILLIS** *comes in.*)

WILLIS. Lesha doll. Didn't I ask you to accompany your mother to the cashier booth?

FELECIA. Yeah, but –

WILLIS. No buts about it. I told you and you defied me, girl.

FERNIE. I'll send it to your room.

WILLIS. You'll send nothing of the kind, Mr. Santos. I'd appreciate your keepin' your hands off my girl from now on.

FERNIE. I didn't touch her.

FELECIA. We were only talking –

WILLIS. I don't know about Nevada, but in my perimeter, there's a statutory age-limit to what a man can stick his pecker to.

FERNIE. Well, in my mind, Casper –

WILLIS. It's not your mind I'm concerned about, mister.

FERNIE. WHY IS EVERYBODY TELLIN' ME WHO TO FUCK!

FELECIA. Please, honey, he wasn't trying anything –

FERNIE. *(Producing his blade from underneath his coat.)* AWRIGHT COWBOY! LET'S TALK!

FELECIA. Oh lord! No! Stop this! Momma! Somebody! Help!

WILLIS. Sonny, put the knife away.

FERNIE. Wanna dance? C'mon, I'll cut a little rug in your two-step, Casper!

WILLIS. Don't make me do this. I just done my time.

FERNIE. Your ass is grass, Hopalong! You fuckin' with the stereotype now!

> **(MIKE** *and* **NENA** *enter.* **PEGGY** *comes from the other side.)*

PEGGY. What the heck's going on here?

FELECIA. Momma, make them stop this! Somebody's gonna get hurt.

NENA. *Fernando! ¡Ya calmate! Aqui no hay para que te pelees.*

PEGGY. Casper, back off. Both of you.

MIKE. Put it away, Negro.

FERNIE. You got no idea who you fuckin' with, asshole! I go back to the Aztecs. I got the blood in my veins, goddammit, I got the face, the features, and I got the disposition of my dyin' race all over me. I'm a spic, man. Beans and tortillas. Through and through.

WILLIS. Honorable ancestry, I'm told.

FERNIE. Damn right.

WILLIS. Goodnight, folks.

> *(The* **WILLISES** *leave.)*

NENA. *¿Estas loco o que? Es un ex-con* and you with a toy knife!

FERNIE. Well, I'm horny!

MIKE. You're real slick.

FERNIE. Sorry, bro. The girl came up, man, I don't know.

MIKE. Fernie, C called. The Feds nailed our horse trailer.

FERNIE. No way!

NENA. The whole shipment.

FERNIE. But how did they...

MIKE. They were tipped off. Someone shit on us, Fernie.

FERNIE. Was there anything tying us to the shit?

MIKE. I don't think so.

FERNIE. Who the fuck told?

NENA. Somebody from the inside, I bet.

MIKE. I can't think about that right now. We're packing for home. I gotta let Tommy know. Negro, I suggest before this night is over, you call your wife.

> (*A phone rings in the darkness.* **VICKY** *and* **TOMAS** *enter her house. She regards the phone.*)

VICKY. There he goes. Checking up on me.

TOMAS. How do you know it's him?

VICKY. By the way it rings. Shrill and whiny.

TOMAS. Maybe you should answer.

> (*The phone stops ringing.*)

VICKY. Coors or Corona?

TOMAS. Coors.

> (*As* **VICKY** *goes off.*)

[Victoria. As I've always known her. *Victoria mi novia mi nova* my ex. Just as we lost lands, wars, lives, dignity, I lost Victoria. Not Vicky as Fernie wants his wife to be, but Victoria.]

VICKY. (*Returning with two beers.*) I hope you'll let me chip in half for the movie –

TOMAS. My treat, Vick. I don't often get to spend time with Lila and Rose. Hey, this sofa look familiar?

VICKY. It should. It's from the store. Like everything else I got. All our houses look the same inside. Your dad's way of living on.

TOMAS. *(Raising his beer.)* To the flower of the Santos Family.

VICKY. You're a trip.

      (They drink. **VICKY** *takes out her vial of coke.)*

TOMAS. *(As she takes a bump.)* [Pollen on the flower, a pinky-nailful of moondust, and my brothers are with us.]

VICKY. What I said earlier about not remembering
I remember
It took a little effort but you
Know those were crazy times we
Were so caught up in this I don't
know this truly I don't know
like at the levee that night drinking beer and playing tapes and making out while the wetbacks wade across the river and then you say something like –

TOMAS. Victoria any one of them could have been us

VICKY. And it cracks me up 'cause it's true and
I lean on the horn by mistake and all of a sudden everything freezes
the water the reeds the gravel the moonlight the wets all become one
big eye
aimed right at us, you see I do remember 'cause right after that you said –

TOMAS. This night is a part of us.

VICKY. What did we know man
one night does not a life make,
sure we're practically related now,
only not the way we
hey hey hey Tomas don't
I mean hey I I I I

I want to ask you
has Fernie said anything about us having kids
'cause uh-uh we're not
we're not we're not
I'm staying on the pill
till he starts acting like a
married man, for all we know
there might already be some
Fernie Jrs running around
oh yeah I've seen his
nacho-cheese-flavored condoms
it's a drag
D R A G
DRAG try and run the business by yourself, it wears me
out, I get no support, Nena's too busy with her kids and
Mike and Negro are always limmigrating –

TOMAS. Litigating.

VICKY. Yea which as you know
all by myself me I have to do it
I need a break from it see this
My little pick-me-up-and-throw-me-across-the-room
you see what good is memory
it only makes you want to forget.
Am I rambling?

TOMAS. No.

VICKY. You're not saying much. You're keeping something
from me. What?

TOMAS. Vick, those people we saw crossing the river:
they're our moms and dads and they drank dirty water
for us. They died for us. We're the dross of dreams,
Victoria, the dreams of good people who try who still
wish who still believe that all this is still theirs. We owe
them our honesty our courage our love.

VICKY. What is it, Tomas?

TOMAS. I I still feel the same for you only more so.

(They resist the impulse to kiss.)

TOMAS. *(Cont.)* [All night we sit up and talk –

VICKY. Inventing histories between us –

TOMAS. Possibilities in the past and present –

VICKY. Talking –

TOMAS. – on a sofa you made Papa, pulsing toward the north, my Mexican descent, thinking of my brothers, but Vicky says –]

VICKY. Stay as long as you want. They need you, they'll ask for you.

(The office. **MIKE, FERNIE, CAMACHO,** *and* **PAM.** *)*

MIKE. Where is he?

CAMACHO. Looked everywhere.

FERNIE. Did you try his place again?

CAMACHO. Nothing.

MIKE. Pam?

PAM. I called all his buddies. No sign of him.

MIKE. Shit. He missed that appointment with the Savings bunch.

PAM. I'll reschedule.

FERNIE. What the fuck's happened, C?

CAMACHO. Just the seizure. No-one busted.

FERNIE. Maybe one of them narked.

CAMACHO. I know those *vatos*. No way.

MIKE. Was there anything tying us to the shit?

CAMACHO. Not a thing.

MIKE. You sure?

CAMACHO. Sure.

FERNIE. You sure?

CAMACHO. I'm sure.

PAM. The Bureau thinks they have something.

MIKE. How do you know?

PAM. It made CNN, Mike. Everyone knows.

FERNIE. Shit.

MIKE. What is this "something"?

PAM. They didn't say.

FERNIE. They're bluffing.

CAMACHO. There wasn't a hair in the place, Mike.

MIKE. Nothing?

CAMACHO. Absolutely nothing.

PAM. You got a lot of calls on the machine.

MIKE. You got the tape?

PAM. Right here.

> *(**MIKE** smashes it.)*

FERNIE. We're in deep shit.

MIKE. You spent the weekend away and you didn't come in until tomorrow.

PAM. Right.

MIKE. C, go to Vicky's and get her ass over here.

FERNIE. I'll call her.

MIKE. No more phone calls. *(To **CAMACHO**.)* Go.

> *(**CAMACHO** goes. He steps into **VICKY**'s living room and finds them sleeping fully-clothed on the sofa.)*

CAMACHO. Vicky! Hey! – *(Seeing them and turning away.)* Oh shit. Sorry, man.

VICKY. C! Dammit, don't you know how to knock!

CAMACHO. The door was open.

VICKY. Well, come in since you're in.

CAMACHO. Mike wants to see you right away at the office.

VICKY. The office? I thought he was in Vegas!

CAMACHO. They had to come back.

VICKY. What's going on?

CAMACHO. Just hurry. We got some problems.

VICKY. C, what happened?

CAMACHO. Vicky, c'mon.

VICKY. What the hell happened?

CAMACHO. The Feds. I can't say anymore.

VICKY. The Feds?

CAMACHO. I can't say anymore.

> (*As* **VICKY** *goes off to get her purse,* **MIKE**, **FERNIE**, *and* **PAM** *feed documents into a paper shredder.*)

PAM. You want these in there too?

MIKE. I'm talking no chances.

PAM. This is the Land Grant Commission file.

MIKE. Put it in.

FERNIE. Man, this bites.

MIKE. Do me a favor, Pam, bring the other files for me.

> (*She goes.*)

Fernando, I think I know who narked on us.

FERNIE. Who?

MIKE. Think about it. We go to Vegas, he stays behind, no-one to supervise him, no-one to know.

FERNIE. Aw...man. Son of a bitch.

CAMACHO. (*As* **PAM** *returns with the files.*) Hey, Tomas.

> (**TOMAS** *keeps still.*)

Mike and Fernie. Worried about you. Tried to call you all night. Nena's girls, *ese,* they thought something happened to you.

TOMAS. I guess I should see them.

CAMACHO. You should see Mike first.

> (**VICKY** *enters.*)

VICKY. Camacho, I want you to know Tommy and me were only –

CAMACHO. You don't gotta explain nothing. I'm just the fuckin' sprayhead.

> (*They cross into the office.*)

PAM. Well, look who's here.

MIKE. We've been trying to reach you for hours.

VICKY. The answering machine was off. And I overslept.

FERNIE. I'll bet.

MIKE. *¿Y tu?*

CAMACHO. I found him passed out in his car.

FERNIE. You're kidding.

TOMAS. I…uh…pulled a bender.

PAM. Buncha sound sleepers in this burg.

VICKY. C said something about Feds.

MIKE. Well, have you heard? We've been shat upon.

VICKY. What?

FERNIE. Somebody tipped off the fuckin' cops and blew our load. *¡Pero cuando lo agarre, le voy a mochar los pinchi huevos!*

PAM. Would somebody translate that for me, please?

VICKY. He said whoever did this is gonna get his balls cut off.

PAM. Assuming this person has balls.

MIKE. That's what we're gonna find out. Vicky, I want you to go to my home and stay with the girls till we call. Pam, close the office down and get someone to change the locks on the door. The rest of you guys meet me at the city dump at 10:30 tonight. I have to make a few calls. *Vamonos, cabrones.*

> (**PAM, FERNIE,** *and* **CAMACHO** *go.* **MIKE** *turns to* **TOMAS.**)

Tommy, you better show. We know who did this.

> (**MIKE** *goes.*)

VICKY. Is this your handiwork?

TOMAS. I had to do it.

VICKY. Is this what you mean by the dross of dreams? An anonymous tip? Tommy, that's our cash cow!

TOMAS. Well, I just slaughtered it.

VICKY. Jesus Christ, you turned your brothers in to the cops!

TOMAS. Look, it's just their stash.

VICKY. God, you really messed things up. I don't believe you.

TOMAS. Vicky, listen, here's where we remake the past. We can make ourselves new. You remember, like last night when we –

VICKY. Last night meant nothing. All we did was sleep, that's all.

Remember. You're my husband's brother. This is your family.

Do you have any idea what this is leading to?

TOMAS. Yeah. City dump.

> (*Lights change. A pair of piercing headlights.* **VICKY** *and the scenery vanish.* **TOMAS** *remains. Propulsive Texas rock 'n' roll in the style of ZZ Top's "Tush"* plays. Cries off.* **FERNIE** *pushes* **CAMACHO** *on, tied with bungie cord.* **MIKE** *follows with a can of gasoline.*)

FERNIE. (*Dancing wildly around* **CAMACHO**.) YYYAOOW, MAAAANN! BAATTLLE STAAATIOONS! WE GONNA PARTY TONIGHT!

CAMACHO. Fernie…ese…

FERNIE. Shut your ass, motherfucker! You ain't been called on yet!

TOMAS. Mike, what's going on?

MIKE. Yo, C. How ya doin' man?

CAMACHO. Lookit…

MIKE. I know how you feel, bro. It's a bad scene for sure.

---

*A license to produce SANTOS & SANTOS does not include a performance license for TUSH. The publisher and author suggest that the licensee contact ASCAP or BMI to ascertain the music publisher and contact such music publisher to license or acquire permission for performance of the song. If a license or permission is unattainable for TUSH the licensee may not use the song in SANTOS & SANTOS but may create an original composition in a similar style. For further information, please see Music Use Note on page 3.

(**MIKE** *douses him with gasoline.*)

TOMAS. What are you doing, Mikey? This is C, man.

MIKE. I know, Tommy. That's what really hurts.

FERNIE. (*Reeling him around like a roped steer.*) SUMBITCH! YOU RATTED ON THE WRONG PEOPLE, ESE!

CAMACHO. What you talkin' about? I didn't rat!

TOMAS. You got the wrong guy. Camacho would never do a thing like that.

CAMACHO. Never. Never. I love you guys.

MIKE. C, you're a Judas, man. A fuckin' Judas.

FERNIE. After all we did.

CAMACHO. I didn't do shit, Mike. That's the truth.

TOMAS. I believe him.

MIKE. We'll see about that.

FERNIE. (*Poised with a match.*) Awright. Why'd you fink?

CAMACHO. I didn't.

(**FERNIE** *flicks a lit match at* **CAMACHO.**)

NO, MAN!

TOMAS. Hey, c'mon! The guy didn't do it. Fernie, stop it!

FERNIE. You gonna burn motherfucker! Now, how much you get for ratting?

CAMACHO. Nothing!

(**FERNIE** *flicks another match.*)

C'mon, Fernie! Jesus Christ, man!

TOMAS. You're gonna kill him. Let him go!

MIKE. Tommy, you're a man with real heart. That's why I asked you to come.

FERNIE. Are you fucking my wife, C? Are you balling her when I'm gone!

CAMACHO. NO WAY! I wouldn't –

(**FERNIE** *flicks another match.*)

Damn, ese! Watch it!

TOMAS. That's enough! Let him go.

CAMACHO. Tell him, Tomas. Tell him I didn't do none a that shit. Tell him!

FERNIE. Shut your fucking ass! I'm talking to you. If you're not fucking my wife, if you're not snitching on us, then who is?

CAMACHO. I dunno!

TOMAS. It was me. I did it! I'm the one who made the call.

FERNIE. Nice try, bro.

MIKE. We know who's responsible.

TOMAS. I'm the one who snitched. C had nothing to do with it.

FERNIE. Don't be covering for this sack of shit, Tommy!

TOMAS. I'm telling you the truth! Let him go!

MIKE. I've known this *vato* longer than anyone, Tomas. My father brought him in as a brother. But this brother is the only one who knew the horse trailer was at Gila Stables!

CAMACHO. Please! Mike!

> (**WILLIS** *strolls on, carrying a small hand-held propane torch.*)

WILLIS. Evenin' boys. Cold moon comin' out.

FERNIE. What are you doing here?

MIKE. I called him.

TOMAS. Who is this guy?

WILLIS. Casper T. Willis. You must be the kid.

> (*He gives him a cursory frisk with his free hand, snapping a few buttons off.*)

FERNIE. What the fuck are you doing here?

WILLIS. (*Lighting the torch.*) I heard we were lightin' a bonfire.

MIKE. He's going to take care of things.

CAMACHO. Hey, don't come near me with that!

WILLIS. And you must be the bonfire.

CAMACHO. Stay back! Tomas!

TOMAS. Get rid of him! This is between the family!

WILLIS. I sure hope you're paid up on your fire insurance.

CAMACHO. No no…you keep away… Tomas, this guy…no NO!

> *(**CAMACHO** staggers off. **WILLIS** follows calmly behind.)*

FERNIE. HEY!

TOMAS. Miguel, you better stop that fuck!

MIKE. Stay where you are!

> *(The agonized cries of **CAMACHO** being immolated.)*

FERNIE. MOTHER OF GOD. OH JESUS!

MIKE.	**FERNIE.**
GET BACK HERE! GET BACK HERE! *(Etc.)*	CAMACHO! THAT'S OUR BRO!

> *(**TOMAS** is spellbound with horror.)*

MIKE. Let's go, Tomas!

> *(The office. **TOMAS** and **MIKE** are still. **FERNIE** paces anxiously. A long silence.)*

FERNIE. Unbelievable.

MIKE. Sit down.

FERNIE. This is evil. Burning a man alive. *Mi camarada.* Camachito.

MIKE. Sit down.

FERNIE. The matches were wet. We were only gonna scare the guy.

MIKE. Sit down, Negro.

TOMAS. Where did you find the goon? Since when did we start doing business with that element?

MIKE. That element *is* our business.

TOMAS. Oh, just another day at the office, huh?

MIKE. Don't start on me. Camacho was my bud. His blood ran in my veins.

> (*PAM comes in and gives* **MIKE** *a paper.*)

MIKE. *(Cont.)* What's this?

PAM. I'm sorry, Mike. I'm leaving.

MIKE. Bad timing, girl.

FERNIE. C'mon, *esa,* you gotta stick it out.

TOMAS. Let her go if she wants to.

PAM. I'm not going to jail for anyone.

MIKE. Go with my blessing, Pam. Just leave the number of your next of kin with us, okay?

> (*PAM tears the resignation.* **NENA** *and* **VICKY** *enter.* **VICKY** *sits in a state of shock as* **NENA** *opens the gym bag.*)

NENA. *Que paso, cabrones. (No reply.)* I know. *Puta suerte.* Vicky and me, when Mike told us, we cried all night. We're gonna miss Camachito. I hope he really likes Burma.

TOMAS. What are you talking about?

NENA. I looked in the books last night y *encontre un* $25,000 deficit. I went up to his apartmento esta mañana to ask him about it and found this. Receipt from the sale of his bike. Here's the receipt from his plane ticket he bought. Also I found me a big old stash of coke y *una bolsa* he musta forgot with $5,000 at least. He musta knew the heat was coming down *y se arranco a la carrera.*

TOMAS. You framed him.

NENA. Looks to me like we're victims of embezzlement, honey.

MIKE. Son of a bitch better not spend it all on whores.

FERNIE. Nena, you tricky fucking devil woman.

TOMAS. The guy is dead and you framed him.

NENA. *Cuñado,* I got two girls at home. My two pieces of American pie. You see what I'm saying?

PAM. Mike.

> (**WILLIS** *enters. He opens a handkerchief over an ashtray and a cascade of teeth dribble into it.*)

WILLIS. My calling card.

MIKE. What the fuck.

NENA. Those are teeth.

WILLIS. He'll be difficult to identify without 'em.

TOMAS. *(As **FERNIE** rushes out in revulsion.)* Jesus.

MIKE. This is going too far.

WILLIS. I'm doing you a favor. He won't be around if and when a grand jury convenes over this bust.

> *(As he goes from person to person, plucking buttons off.)*

You know, the Bay Breasted Warbler is a lil' thing about this big, dark-looking with a chestnut throat, upper breast. It has a pretty lil' call which goes like "tees teesi teesi." The Cape May Warbler, though, comes in yellow and sounds higher and thinner like "seet seet seet seet." My favorite is the common yellowthroat which has a black mask like the Lone Ranger and a bright rapid chant that goes "Witchy-witchy-witchy witch. Witchy-witchy-witchy witch." I love birds, you see. I go to all parts to find them. But one bird I do not like is the pigeon. It has no grace, it has no beauty, it has no song but the song of betrayal.

PAM. *(As **WILLIS** approaches her.)* Don't even think about it.

WILLIS. *(Turning to **MIKE**.)* Cash is what we discussed.

NENA. Here it is. The twenty grand Camacho's blowin' in Burma.

WILLIS. Count it.

NENA. I have

WILLIS. Again.

NENA. I have.

WILLIS. Mr. Santos, you have some pig-headed women on your team. That's good. *Hasta luego.*

> *(**WILLIS** leaves with the gym bag.)*

NENA. Asshole.

PAM. I second that.

TOMAS. What ungodly jam are we in now, Mike?

MIKE. It's over.

TOMAS. We gotta get rid of those teeth.

> (**MIKE** *dumps them into* **TOMAS***'s pocket.* **FERNIE** *returns.*)

FERNIE. Is he gone?

MIKE. Yeah, freak.

FERNIE. I'll kill him next time, Mike. I swear it.

NENA. Won't be no next time.

PAM. Mike, I think after all this crap, you owe us a pizza.

MIKE. Best idea yet. I'm starved. Let's go.

NENA. Fernie's treat!

FERNIE. No way! Your turn! I paid for the gasoline!

> (*They exit.* **VICKY** *and* **TOMAS** *remain. Silence.*)

TOMAS. They…killed him.

VICKY. They?

TOMAS. He was…sss…set…on fire…

VICKY. Tommy…don't you dare…

TOMAS. I…have his…teeth…

VICKY. (*Lunging at him with her fists.*) DON'T YOU DARE CRY, YOU CHICKEN SHIT! YOU FUCK! YOU GOT NO RIGHT TO CRY! YOU COULD HAVE SAVED HIM! YOU COULD HAVE SAID SOMETHING!

TOMAS. I did! I told them!

VICKY. (*Falling to her knees in sobs.*) YOU LET HIM DIE! FUCK YOU, TOMMY! FUCK YOU! YOU BURNED HIM!

TOMAS. [I did it for us, for our people's sake, I saw Camacho flare like a sun, Papa, like an emanation of *EL Corazón*, I saw him blazing with justice AND IT WAS GLORIOUS!]

> (*Tableau. Screaming sirens. Blackout.*)

End of Act I

ACT II

> (**TOMAS** *enters amid smoke and darkness,*
> *searching.* **CAMACHO** *emerges from the shadows.*)

TOMAS. [CAMACHO! CAMACHO…! C? C, is that you?

CAMACHO. *Vato.* What brings you to this dump?

TOMAS. I came to bury you, man.

CAMACHO. Not a chance, *ese.* Ain't nothin' left to bury.

TOMAS. Shit. I'm really sorry, C.

CAMACHO. Don't cry. The Santos brothers are men of honor. What's up?

TOMAS. Mike got busted at the pizza parlor. He's to be formally charged. Fernie got so worked up, he copped a feel from Pam. She stuck him with a ballpoint.

CAMACHO. I warned that dude.

TOMAS. C, I don't get it. I don't understand what killed you, my brothers' law or the law of the land.

CAMACHO. *(Revealing a tape measurer.)* What's the point? They both kill.

TOMAS. What's that for?

> *(From off, the voice of* **DON MIGUEL.**)

DON MIGUEL. *Camacho!*

CAMACHO. *Aqui!*

> (**DON MIGUEL** *appears.*)

TOMAS. *Papa.*

DON MIGUEL. *¿Listo? Los* dimensions got to be perfect.

> (**CAMACHO** *measures out an oblong space on the*
> *floor.*)

It's gonna be a special piece. Me and this lumber *venimos de Concordia.*

TOMAS. *Mi padre, mi padre, mi patria.*

DON MIGUEL. I miss the old town. I was a *chavo* of seventeen when I left. Nothing to it but a plaza, a church, and some open pavilions filled with woodwork. But it was home to me.

TOMAS. Forgive us our chicanismo, our only begotten sin.

DON MIGUEL. All my life I have wanted to go back. But no: my family is here, my work, and my life. A measure of grace awaits me.

TOMAS. Grant us *amnestia mi padre.*

CAMACHO. Don Miguel, I finished the measurements.

DON MIGUEL. *¿Ya?* Then let's go work on it.

> (*Showing* **TOMAS** *his tattoo.*)

Misericordia, Tomas.

> (*They recede into the thick smoke as the sound of hammers pounding echoes inside* **TOMAS**.)

TOMAS. *¡Misericordia mis hermanos mi padre mi padre mi padre!]*

> (*Flash bulbs explode all around him and intense white light comes on his face.* **TOMAS** *addresses "the Press."*)

This family's honor is unimpeachable! My brother has done nothing wrong!

> (*He goes. In the foreground the* **WILLIS** *family watch TV as the others rush around. Garish camera lighting and flashbulbs.*)

PEGGY. Honey, lookit this! Michael's all over the ten o'clock!

WILLIS. Yeah, I see him.

MIKE. No comment. Please relay all questions to my attorney. No sir. No comment –

FERNIE. As my brother's attorney, I'll move that the charges be dismissed on the grounds of unlawful arrest and insufficient evidence –

GONZALEZ. John Gonzalez from the US Attorney's office. We've charged Mr. Santos with racketeering, illegal gambling, conspiracy to possess and distribute illegal narcotics, and failure to renew his Texas driver's license –

NENA. I don't like the look of that Gonzalez man. He's got a mean face.

GONZALEZ. Members of the Press, Miguel Santos has been arraigned.

FELECIA. Pappy, what's arraign?

WILLIS. Water comes from the sky.

FELECIA. You think you're funny.

JUDGE. That's right. I have just received the news that Michael Santos will be tried in my court in San Antonio. –

TOMAS. What? Benton? Judge Benton is trying my own brother?!

GONZALEZ. Today we invoked the Kingpin Statute against Mr. Santos –

FERNIE. Hey! Dirty pool!

JUDGE. Continuing criminal enterprise. Mandatory life sentence with no parole –

MIKE. No comment. No comment. Excuse me. Excuse me. No comment –

WILLIS. Ladies, Christmas comes a little early this year.

*(He gives **FELECIA** a pretty necklace.)*

FELECIA. Pappy! Are they diamonds?

WILLIS. Yep. And this is for you, darlin'

*(He gives **PEGGY** a pearl-handled revolver.)*

PEGGY. Damn, Casper, this is Christmas.

GONZALEZ. Our investigation has revealed sinister connections with the Colombian cartels and powerful underworld elements in Las Vegas –

VICKY. The only Colombian connection Mike has is with coffee –

TOMAS. I am personally mobilizing the family resources for Mike's bail. He's not spending another night in jail.

GONZALEZ. I've persuaded the local magistrate to set bond at five million.

VICKY. Five million! It's outrageous!

GONZALEZ. We've moved the opening trial date to April sixth –

FERNIE. You can't do that! BB King's playing the Sands that night, man –

NENA. I have begun a three-day fast in protest of my husband's arrest.

MIKE. No comment. No comment. I'm not saying a word. No comment –

PEGGY. That Juarez dirt trash has no business with Mikey.

FELECIA. Pappy, can I have some cocaine?

WILLIS. Babydoll, you know I don't like you doing that stuff before bedtime –

FERNIE. It's clear to me that the US Attorney's office has had extensive carnal knowledge of the bench Judge Benton is sitting on –

JUDGE. I deeply resent any aspersions cast upon the integrity of this court. Mr. Santos' comments are not only out of line with the ABA's code of ethics, but show clear contempt for the rules of this judiciary –

PEGGY. *(Firing at the judge.)* Pphhrr! Say hi to Jesus, Judge!

NENA. They got the wrong guy. That's what I have to say.

PEGGY. *(Firing at* **NENA.** *)* Pphhrr! You too, Tia Maria!

GONZALEZ. We're looking for Jesus Camacho, a bandido Motorcycle Club member and a Santos associate who disappeared recently –

MIKE. No comment. I have no comment. No comment –

FELECIA. They're gonna nail 'im, huh, Pappy?

WILLIS. Hell, they haven't even found the charred body yet.

PEGGY. What charred body, Casper?

TOMAS. My brother will be absolved before God. I have faith in both our family and in the American Legal System –

> (*The* **JUDGE** *strips off his robe, revealing a tennis outfit. He produces a tennis racket.* **FERNIE** *stands holding a brief as if at a hearing.*)

FERNIE. I move that bond for my client be reduced to 500,000.

JUDGE. (*Swinging his racket with each reply.*) Motion denied.

FERNIE. I moved for a continuance until further –

JUDGE/GONZALEZ. Motion denied.

FERNIE. I move for a change of venue on the grounds of –

JUDGE/GONZALEZ/TOMAS. Motion denied.

FERNIE. I move that the judge recuse himself on the basis of prejudicial evidence!

NENA/JUDGE/GONZALEZ/TOMAS/VICKY. Motion denied!

FERNIE. SHIT!

> (*Everyone clears except for the* **WILLISES.**)

FELECIA. Can you put this on for me, Pappy?

WILLIS. 'Course, honey.

PEGGY. Why don't you put on some clothes while you're at it? You're a lady, not a call girl.

FELECIA. Are you bein' spiteful just 'cause I got a chain and you didn't?

PEGGY. I got a gun, Felecia Lee. Don't make me use it.

> (**PEGGY** *leaves.*)

FELECIA. Whoo-ee. Who peed in her popcorn?

WILLIS. C'mon. Time for bed, eiderduck.

FELECIA. Will you come and tuck me in, Pappy?

WILLIS. Honey, it's my life's abidin' pleasure.

> (*They go. Lights up on two chairs and a table.* **MIKE,** *looking weary and unfocused, and* **FERNIE.**)

FERNIE. Fuckin' redneck judge, he hates your guts.

MIKE. What do they have?

FERNIE. The horse trailer. C bought it in your name.

MIKE. Fuck. Nena?

FERNIE. Startin' to show. She's a rock. Tommy's okay, too. I got him digging through the US Attorney's files for the evidentiary hearing.

MIKE. He's good.

FERNIE. Tommy?

MIKE. US Attorney.

FERNIE. Fuckin' sellout if you ask me. He puts on a nice suit, gets a job with the government and thinks he's white as rice. How are you doing?

MIKE. Like shit. I haven't slept a wink since I got in. Next time you come back, make sure you bring Tommy.

FERNIE. What for?

MIKE. I want to see him.

(*The Law Office. With* TOMAS.)

TOMAS. But what for?

FERNIE. He said he wants to see you.

TOMAS. Look, can't you tell him that I'm already doing what I can? I'm doing my best, Fernie, I really am.

FERNIE. He wouldn't ask for you if it weren't important.

TOMAS. I hate jails. I don't like coming near them.

FERNIE. If you're gonna be a criminal lawyer you better get used to it. Mira, Tomas, I'm not gonna argue with you. Mikey said he wants you to come with next time, *me entiendes?* So you come with.

(**FERNIE** *exits as* **VICKY** *enters.*)

VICKY. He's your brother. You haven't laid eyes on him since the arrest.

TOMAS. I can't go into jails. Those faces in there. Staring back at me. Giving me those looks.

VICKY. You've got to get over that, Tommy. The past is the past.

TOMAS. How can you say that? You were closer to Camacho than anyone.

VICKY. I know. That's what got him killed. From now on, Tommy, we have to know better. We've got to be cutthroats or we're dead.

TOMAS. I'm not double-crossing anyone.

VICKY. Then why did you rat?

TOMAS. I had to do something. I saw what the family was becoming. You said I was a Santos, but I don't know what that means anymore.

VICKY. Nobody's blaming you, Tommy. The damage was done way before you came. *(She kisses him.)* I lied when I told you that night didn't mean anything. You made my house more bearable by staying in it.

TOMAS. Your hands are shaking.

VICKY. Fernie said we shouldn't have any drugs in the house while the investigation is going on. Easy for him to say.

TOMAS. I could...score something for you.

VICKY. Don't mess up again. You're still the cream of the family.

> *(They kiss again as* **MIKE** *bellows from his table.)*

MIKE. TOMMY! TOMMY! TOMMY! TOMMY! TOMMY! TOMMY!

> *(***VICKY** *breaks away and goes.* **TOMAS** *turns toward* **MIKE***.)*

TOMAS. You got sucrose eyes, Mike.

MIKE. I don't sleep. If I sleep, I dream. I see smoke and fire. School desks around me. Burning. Camacho and my girls are charred black.

TOMAS. We're going to get you out. Soon as we raise bail. Quit worrying and get some rest, *carnal.*

MIKE. Why did you protect him? He was the one who narked, wasn't he?

TOMAS. He was a friend.

MIKE. I know. I know. Camachito. What do I do now?

TOMAS. Plead guilty.

MIKE. This is my fucking defense?

TOMAS. They've rejected every motion Negro's made, denied us access to the evidence and witnesses, and this judge wants you to do major time. Now, we can knock off a few years by pleading guilty on the lesser charges. You won't look unrepentant, you won't perjure yourself. You'll get ten, but you'll do seven, maybe six with good behavior. Hell, with the overcrowding nowadays, you may get out in four. The thing is you're gonna do time.

MIKE. How many of us have you fed this line to?

TOMAS. Some other judge might give you a shot, but Benton won't recuse himself.

MIKE. What if we get someone to recuse his ass for him?

TOMAS. I don't follow you.

MIKE. What if he goes down before trial?

TOMAS. Goes down?

MIKE. I'll do anything to get out, Tommy.

TOMAS. I don't even want to hear this. You're not proposing what I think you are. We go by our procedure, we trust the legal process.

MIKE. We lost faith in that a long time ago, brother.

TOMAS. Don't talk about this, Mike. It's perverse. I won't have any part of it.

MIKE. *Bueno.*

TOMAS. Is this why you wanted to see me?

MIKE. I just wondered how far you would go for us.

    (**MIKE** *teeters off.*)

TOMAS. [*Servicio,* the will to do service, *servicio del corazón,* Papa, to do, to do in, to do in vain, to act for the heart…the heart…]

*(A dark street. The **JUDGE** steps out in an overcoat.)*

JUDGE. You come alone?

TOMAS. Yes.

JUDGE. I think often of our talk. Your vision impressed me.

TOMAS. What is it you want?

JUDGE. I come to you a divided man. My involvement in the case of The People vs. Michael Santos distresses me. A part of me urges me toward my duty and a part urges me toward you. We share the burden now.

TOMAS. My brother is no burden.

JUDGE. It's more than just him, Tomas. That evening in the parking lot, you returned something to me. Something I tried to beat back my whole life. Paloma's boy. My son, who lives in the faces of those in my court. I love you deeply troubled people, I long for you as passionately as you long for justice.

TOMAS. Then recuse yourself.

JUDGE. No. I'm going to try Michael Santos under the sign of El Broken Heart just as you would.

TOMAS. I want nothing to do with you! You used me! You used me to get to my brothers! You don't love us! You want to hang us! You made me turn them in!

JUDGE. I knew it was you. Only the good son.

TOMAS. You used me so you could try him in that kennel you call the court!

JUDGE. I may be trying him, but by God, you've already judged him. In your heart, he's guilty. A dealer, a crook, a liar, a thief, a traitor, possibly even a killer. But the sin you damn him for is being Mexican. Right, Tommy? We're a pair, you and me; I loathe your kind 'cause I love them, and you love them to bury your loathing.

TOMAS. You're a sick old man, you can't see into my soul, my soul is mine, this garbage is my garbage! Keep away from me!

JUDGE. We're going to try him by your symbol before a jury of his peers, twelve three-headed versions of you, twelve manifest destinies, and YOU Tomas, my boy my son YOU will be the star witness the informant the good son with the vision here here –

(Taking off his coat and rolling back his sleeve.)

The whole enchilada the grandest proof see see here on my arm I have the Sign too! The gringo has a miracle!

(He reveals the heart tattooed on his forearm.)

We shall convict him with one *corazón* beating between us, bu-bum bu-bum bu-bum, *El Corazon Americano!*

(The JUDGE goes. NENA appears.)

TOMAS. [Peace now. *Paz.* El Paso. Everything agrees. Everything fails but family. My brother. My heart. Blood woos me to blood and it agrees.]

NENA. Tommy.

TOMAS. We're going to blow the Judge's brains out.

NENA. This is due process? I thought only in Colombia they did this.

TOMAS. Mike wants it.

NENA. *Estamos bien fregados. Bueno pues,* when do we bail him out?

TOMAS. We're not going for bail.

NENA. *¿Que que?* What do you mean we're not going for the bail?

TOMAS. We need the money for the contract.

NENA. No. No way. No. No, Tomas. Eso no.

TOMAS. *Nena, escuchame –*

NENA. No! I want Miguel out! I want him out!

TOMAS. Will you listen to me! Benton's sending him up whether we get bail or not. I know how you feel, but this is how he wants it. The Judge is a vindictive old crow with a heart full of nails and he has to go.

NENA. You don't even know him and already you're planning to kill him.

TOMAS. I know him, Nena. Better than I know myself. You have the cash from the Colombian deal?

NENA. *Negro lo tiene.* Two million and a half.

TOMAS. We don't tell him anything. This is between you, me, Mike…*y una persona mas.*

> *(They go. **WILLIS** in camouflage jacket, peering through binoculars. **FELECIA** creeps in quietly behind him.)*

FELECIA. Pappy…

WILLIS. Shhh… Slowly…over there…among the reeds…a tricolored heron…very rare for these parts…

FELECIA. Where?

WILLIS. Oh, never mind. You scared it off. What's up, darlin'?

FELECIA. Momma said to bring you this.

> *(She gives him a note. He reads it.)*

WILLIS. Well, this is interestin'.

FELECIA. What's it say?

WILLIS. I can't tell you, Lesha doll. You might be wired.

FELECIA. You can trust me, Pappy.

WILLIS. Sure I can, but in your lamblike innocence, you might be picking up everything I say.

FELECIA. Well, then go ahead if you think I'm bugged.

> *(She stands with her hands raised. **WILLIS** pauses, then frisks her. He picks all the buttons from her clothes.)*

Satisfied?

WILLIS. Your mamma's not gonna like this one bit.

FELECIA. She doesn't have to know, does she?

> *(He slips his hands underneath her clothes and kisses her. They go. **FERNIE** and **PAM** in the*

office with briefs, laptops, etc., as the **JUDGE** *and* **GONZALEZ** *enter.)*

JUDGE. What's wrong, Gomez? Come up against some snags?

GONZALEZ. No sir. The Defense is in a tailspin. But I need to grant a couple of slimeballs clemency in exchange for their testimony.

JUDGE. Real dirtbags?

GONZALEZ. Career scum.

JUDGE. Permission granted. But bump 'em outa my state, you understand?
Send them to Arkansas.

GONZALEZ. I've also empaneled a Special Grand Jury and I need your sayso to broaden their powers some.

JUDGE. Meaning?

GONZALEZ. Wiretap.

JUDGE. By all mean, Ramirez.

GONZALEZ. Could you possibly make this ruling retroactive?

JUDGE. You're bugging them already?

GONZALEZ. *(Producing a recorder.)* Discreet surveillance. We don't want to violate attorney-client confidentiality.

JUDGE. That's not the way we do things around here. Procedure is respected.

GONZALEZ. Well, I thought –

JUDGE. I'm aware of the fact that you're using me to get your plum assignments. Just use me sparingly.

GONZALEZ. I'm on your team, sir.

(**GONZALEZ** *offers the tape player to the* **JUDGE,** *who turns it on. In the office,* **PAM** *and* **FERNIE.** *)*

FERNIE. Awright. They're due any minute. Let's get out those files.

PAM. Got them.

FERNIE. Press packets.

PAM. Check.

FERNIE. Judge's profile.

PAM. Check.

FERNIE. Trial itinerary.

PAM. Check.

FERNIE. Tictacs.

PAM. Check.

FERNIE. Gimme some. I got the breath of a truck.

GONZALEZ. That's Fernie. The woman works there.

FERNIE. Okay, Pam, lemme ask you somethin': how come you're sticking your honky neck out for us like this?

PAM. Didn't you hear what Mike said? Next of kin.

FERNIE. Awright, fuck what Mike said. Far as I'm concerned, walk out now, you walk out free, no trouble.

PAM. Are you serious?

(He nods. She thinks about it.)

No can do, Fernie. I'm like Camacho. You guys are all the family I got left. I'm beginning to feel what you're fighting for.

FERNIE. *Coraje.* Anger.

PAM. I'm talking about something else. Something deeper.

FERNIE. That's the thing about you, Pam. You may be a *gringa lesbo* with an attitude, but you got *huevos.*

PAM. I hear you do too.

GONZALEZ. This is where it gets interesting.

*(**TOMAS, VICKY,** and **NENA** enter.)*

NENA. This better be good, calling a meeting at ten o'clock at night.

TOMAS. Fernando, we need to talk about the Arm and Hammer cut.

FERNIE. Not now. Take a seat. Doin' okay, babe?

VICKY. Ran out of gas. You wouldn't have a gallon around, would you?

FERNIE. Don't be so wise, Vicky.

VICKY. Don't you ever run out of gas?

FERNIE. Only thing I run out of is patience.

NENA. Can we get this going? I left the girls at home by themselves.

VICKY. Hi, Tommy. Why such a stranger lately?

*(**PAM** passes out folders for everyone.)*

FERNIE. We been hashing this out all week and here's the deal. I drafted a statement for every member of the family to say whenever the stupid press gets in our face. Everybody from the local paper to *El Fronterizo* to fucking 20/20.

PAM. We have to watch our backs from now on. The IRS is auditing our books. Files have been confiscated. Bank accounts. Another thing: the phones may be bugged. We can't talk about this or anything related with dear old Ma Bell. Children included.

TOMAS. You really want us to say this to the press about him?

FERNIE. We're mounting a united front against these assholes.

TOMAS. Fernie, you're saying he's framed Mike for being Mexican.

FERNIE. He sent a guy up for ten for possessing two lousy joints. Another got seven for having a crack pipe. And here's one got twenty to life for a few lousy marijuana plants in his backyard. Know what they got in common? Marquez, Martinez, Huerta. Sons of Moctezuma.

JUDGE. Who's he talking about?

GONZALEZ. You.

FERNIE. I've researched this racist, and *vatos*, it's ugly. Benton has buddies in the Congress, the White House, the Bohemian Grove and the Trilateral Commission. He's just a little *moco* in the bigger conspiracy! I'm talking ongoing colonial imperialism for our *pinchi* souls, man! Drugs are the 21st Century Conquistadores! Mikey is a victim of the International Narcotics Trade! A huge motherfucking enterprise that can't be done without

The CIA

The FBI

The DEA

The INS.

And even the Holy Church, which has realized that the opiate of the masses is OPIUM. This underground network fans out to the Texas Bar Association, the ACLU, IBM, and the Men's Wearhouse! Everybody is trying to bone us, *chavos*, like they bone us every time, 'cause let's face it, they're afraid of us, man, we represent an empire!

VICKY. Don't you think you're being a little paranoid, Negro?

FERNIE. *¡La neta!* We gotta get Mike out. That means bail.

> (**FERNIE** *removes his jewelry and puts it on the table.*)

TOMAS. What the hell is this?

FERNIE. Everybody. Ante up. All your fucking jewelry on the table. *Ahora mismo.* Prob'ly enough gold on us to buy a racehorse.

VICKY. You've got to be kidding.

FERNIE. Uh-uh. Balls to the wall. You too, Pam.

PAM. Hey, I'm not family.

TOMAS. Hold it! You're not gonna raise the cash this way.

FERNIE. *(Grabbing* **VICKY**'s *car keys and slamming then on the table.)* Right. Then we put the car up too.

VICKY. That's my car!

FERNIE. It's out of gas, anyway, right?

PAM. Why don't you put up your car?

FERNIE. Yo, I got an image to uphold. Who's gonna trust a lawyer in a late model piece of shit?

VICKY. Depends. Is he in it or under it?

TOMAS. What about the money from the deal?

FERNIE. What deal?

TOMAS. The baking soda deal. There was over two mil. Where's that money?

FERNIE. We don't got that money. It's gone.

TOMAS. What do you mean, it's gone?

FERNIE. Forget it. It's gone, it's spent.

VICKY. You mean, gambled.

FERNIE. I mean, it's gone. End of discussion.

TOMAS. Dammit, Negro, are you saying you blew that money on the tables?

FERNIE. Lookit. We do the best we can. Vicky and me got this nest-egg, IRAs of 150, 160 grand. We'll put it up on our end, okay?

VICKY. Those are the savings for our baby.

FERNIE. What baby? I mean, let's not kid ourselves, Vicky.

NENA. Excuse me one fuckin' minute. What am I here, a smurf?

FERNIE. No, course not, Nena, you got as much –

NENA. I feel like most of these decisions been made by you already. Now, I got great respect for you, *cuñado*, but this business is –

FERNIE. Yes, Nena, I see your point –

NENA. I don't fuckin' think so. My point is I left my two children in an empty house to sit here and listen to your bullshit and I'm getting way pissed off. Negro, *a mi no me vas a maderiar.* First of all, Tommy's right, this statement *es pura mierda*. It will hurt Miguel, bad. Do not fuck with the Judge. And don't think I'm gonna give up my jewelry and my car for some stupid bail, either! You may not have kids, *compa*, but I do, and I ain't giving up not a damn thing. Why don't you try DROPPING THE *PINCHI* DICE FOR A SECOND AND DOING YOUR JOB! By the way, *muñeca*, I know you're only doing your job and Mikey really appreciates you, but you don't tell me or my girls how to use my phone. I'm not your secretary.

<table>
<tr><td>

FERNIE.
Hey, you watch how you
talk to her!

</td><td>

PAM.
Lady, you don't pay my
salary, remember that!

</td></tr>
<tr><td>

NENA.
I'll talk to her any
fucking way I please!

</td><td>

VICKY.
Hey! Hey! C'mon!

</td></tr>
</table>

 (**TOMAS** *slams his fist down. Everyone falls silent.*)

TOMAS. This is not the Santos family. This is a fucking JOKE. Who can blame the Feds for circling over us? Nena, go see to your girls. Negro, do us a favor, get off Benton's case and get on my brother's. Everyone stands by the tribe. *¿Estan de acuerdo?*

 (**NENA** *goes.*)

VICKY. I'll catch a ride with her since I no longer have a car. Oh. Here's something else for your defense fund.

 (**VICKY** *puts her wedding ring in the pile and goes.*)

TOMAS. If you knew how badly we needed that money.

 (**TOMAS** *leaves.* **FERNIE** *and* **PAM** *remain still.*)

JUDGE. (*Snapping the recorder shut.*) Those high-talking Santos bastards, goddamn wetback crud, where do they get off calling me racist! I been on that docket longer than Jesus Christ, an' no-one's been as fair! I've redrawn district lines all over this state to make voting blocs equal! I've made appointments! Black, Women, Jews, Spanish! Racist! By God!

GONZALEZ. When this investigation is through, we'll have something on everyone, including Tomas.

JUDGE. No. I don't want him touched. The others are yours for the taking, but Tommy Santos you leave alone. You understand?

GONZALEZ. If that's the way you really want it –

JUDGE. That's the way I want it.

 (*They go.* **FERNIE** *and* **PAM** *finally stir.*)

PAM. Not so good, huh?

FERNIE. My own brother.

PAM. These are tense times, Fern.

FERNIE. Fuck.

PAM. Don't worry.

FERNIE. I worry.

PAM. You're still the man.

FERNIE. Fuck.

PAM. Going home?

FERNIE. To what?

PAM. Vicky.

FERNIE. Shit. I don't know what's come over her. I useta touch her and burn my hand on her hood. But the last time I had her in bed, I saw the damage of indifference in her face and it sent chills down my ass.

PAM. Then lemme buy you a drink.

FERNIE. Uh-uh. I ain't goin' in no dyke bar.

PAM. Fernie, I ain't no dyke.

FERNIE. Wait a minute. Wait a minute. You're a dyke. You said –

PAM. I said I didn't care for little boys.

FERNIE. Whoa! I don't believe it! You psyched me! You actually psyched me! You are not a dyke!

PAM. Are we going for that drink or what?

(Crossfade to **MIKE** *and* **NENA**.*)*

NENA. *Oye, Viejo.* Sleeping any better?

MIKE. The tears…have grown over my eyes…

NENA. Miguel –

MIKE. My girls' names… I can't remember their names…

NENA. Tomas took money from the scholarship fund for this *desmadre.* Is this how you want things to be?

MIKE. Things are, Nena. You grow up, you marry, you raise kids, you light a match, you burn a man.

NENA. The other day, waiting for the elevator in the courthouse, Gonzalez came up to me.

(**GONZALEZ** *enters and stands by her.*)

GONZALEZ. Señora Santos.

NENA. Don't talk to me. I don't got my lawyer.

GONZALEZ. I just want to say that I tried to turn down the assignment when it was presented to me. This shouldn't happen between Latinos.

NENA. Señor, I come from *La Colonia,* the poorest barrio in Juarez. The streets ain't paved, there's no *luz,* no *gas,* no running water. When I got married, I got me a big fuckin' car and a house and two wonderful girls. The local chicks look down their nose at me, but I could give a shit. I take a bath in real porcelain, my floors got real marble, my girls speak perfect English. I'm a *pinchi* American now. No fuckin' lawyer's taking that away from me.

GONZALEZ. This one's going down. I'm going up.

(**GONZALEZ** *leaves.* **NENA** *turns to* **MIKE.**)

NENA. It's going to be a boy. We're having a son.

(**NENA** *turns.* **PEGGY** *and* **TOMAS** *are waiting.* **TOMAS** *carries a small bag.*)

PEGGY. I need to see your purse.

NENA. What for?

PEGGY. Procedure.

(**NENA** *gives her the purse.* **PEGGY** *searches it.*)

NENA. It sure is hot.

PEGGY. Sure is.

NENA. Do you have any, like, iced tea?

PEGGY. Uh-uh. (*Tossing the purse back.*) We don't got crumpets neither.

(**WILLIS** *enters.*)

WILLIS. Ma'am. *(To* **PEGGY**.*)* Handbag? *(***PEGGY** *nods.)* Folks, I'm not one for small talk. Can we cut to the main artery?

NENA. Señor, my husband would like you to do for him a job.

WILLIS. You want the Honorable William L. Benton whacked. That it?

NENA. Humanely if possible.

WILLIS. He's Federal, you know.

NENA. My husband wants it done.

WILLIS. Sure he does.

NENA. He said you would do him any favor.

WILLIS. That's what I said.

PEGGY. A favor is one thing, missy: this is something else. This is a judge. My honey just spent ten years in the pen. You want to send him to the chair too?

NENA. I was talking to Mr. Willis.

PEGGY. Well you're talking to me now. I watch out for my man, you see. I'm not like some people who let their good men stew in prison. You take your offer elsewhere.

NENA. We can pay.

PEGGY. Don't do it, Casper.

WILLIS. Kid, what's *your* opinion on the matter?

TOMAS. I'm with her. I don't think you should do it either.

NENA. Shut your mouth, Tommy.

WILLIS. Why not?

TOMAS. It's too hard. You'd never get close enough to do it, and if you did, you wouldn't get away with it. You'd blow it for all of us.

WILLIS. You don't know much about me, do you?

TOMAS. I know you did time, which means you were stupid enough to get caught somewhere along the line. Once you fuck up, you fuck up again, and then again, until it becomes part of your M.O. This job can't be done unless it's done right. You may have been the man for a poor defenseless fuck like Camacho, but you're not the gun for this job.

WILLIS. Maybe nobody is.

TOMAS. Then I'll do it myself. I'll whip up the meanest combination dish and force-feed it to him till he croaks of Montezuma's Revenge.

(**WILLIS** *gets up and crosses to* **TOMAS.** *Glares at him.*)

WILLIS. Consider him whacked.

TOMAS. Commission.

WILLIS. Hundred grand. Up front.

TOMAS. *(Tossing him a bag of cash.)* Ten up front. The rest after.

WILLIS. *(Tossing the bag to* **PEGGY.***)* I don't work that way.

TOMAS. Make this an exception.

(**WILLIS** *considers this as* **PEGGY** *counts the cash.*)

WILLIS. I choose the date, location, and method.

TOMAS. Just keep us apprised.

WILLIS. I want a guarantee of secrecy.

TOMAS. Granted.

WILLIS. I'll need his address, color and make of car, recent photos of him and family members.

TOMAS. No problem.

WILLIS. A schedule of his daily and weekly routine, caseload, lunch breaks, appointments, and so forth.

TOMAS. You'll have it next week.

WILLIS. No backing out after today.

TOMAS. It goes both ways.

WILLIS. And I deal with one person only and only one.

TOMAS. You deal with me.

PEGGY. It's all here. Ten thou.

WILLIS. Mrs. Santos, you can tell your husband to ease his soul.

NENA. He goes to trial April sixth.

(Everyone leaves but **TOMAS**.*)*

TOMAS. [Pay money and someone dies. Respect. Power. I am the FBI, CIA, all the governments, their armed forces, Wall Street, the Mob, the High Court, and the Holy Ghost of the Mother Church. I am power. Money is justice. Good money is death.]

*(*TOMAS* goes.* VICKY *packs an open suitcase.* NENA *stands over her.)*

VICKY. Make it fast, Nena. I'm busy.

NENA. Where are you going?

VICKY. Mexico. What is it?

NENA. *(Holding out* **VICKY***'s ring.)* You left this at the office.

VICKY. I don't want it.

NENA. Here.

VICKY. No keep it.

NENA. It's yours, *Victoria*.

VICKY. [Mine what's mine what's the point there's no future no *mañana* everything comes hasta *mañana* as if *mañana* could make everything right.]

NENA. He's an asshole, but he's your husband.

VICKY. [No *mañana* no baby no baby room no hope so what? Hope is a chain hope is our sickness our hell.]

NENA. You made your vows to him.

VICKY. I said no! Listen to me, Nena! I've had it with Santos & Santos! I'm sick of the store, the furniture, the house, I'm through with this shit.

NENA. You got to see past this, see your way through to the things that make life good.

VICKY. What? BMWs? Wide-screen TVs? Designer shoes?

NENA. What's wrong with that? Back where I come from, we didn't even have shoes. Now I got thirty pairs.

VICKY. So do I, Nena. They just don't mean as much to me.

NENA. They would, if you had children –

VICKY. I knew you were going to say that.

NENA. It's the truth. Once my babies came, everything changed. I began to care for the quality of things, to want the best for –

VICKY. Don't lecture me about your kids. I know what you're bringing them up to be. Good for you, Nena, just make sure they don't find out their mommy's Juarez trash.

NENA. *¿Y tu? ¿Que eres tu?* A born stuck-up bitch with only a birthright to be proud of. American chick. Big Deal. You're not whiter than I am. You just act like it. Too good for the things that dazzle us. Go to Mexico, see how they treat you there. You think I got it bad here, there you're worse than a *pinchi gringa.* Lookit you now. Lookit you.

VICKY. What happened to me? I was something. I was like PROMISED this great life. I thought I could ride high on the Santos name. I thought oh god I was something.

NENA. *Ay, mijita.* Better get your ass clean right away and hold on to this.

> *(Placing the ring in her hand.)*

Our kids deserve a chance to fuck up their lives, too, don't they?

> *(**NENA** goes. **TOMAS** has been watching as she stands over her open suitcase.)*

VICKY. [Hope is our only possible hell.]

TOMAS. Hi.

VICKY. I must have left ten messages on your machine.

TOMAS. Sorry. I was out of town. Vicky, I need some money.

VICKY. Why ask me? Negro's the one with the cash.

TOMAS. The furniture store's in your name. You could go to the bank and borrow against the store. I need at least 90,000.

VICKY. *¿Para que?* Are you in trouble? *(No response.)* That's your father's store. His soul is in it.

TOMAS. You don't have to tell me that.

VICKY. What's happening to you? Why are you keeping yourself from me?

TOMAS. Vicky, don't ask me any questions. Just I need the money.

VICKY. Look at us, Tommy. A couple of scarecrows with all our needs coming out at the seams. Is this what we wanted to be?

TOMAS. Your phone's ringing.

(**FERNIE**, *naked, draped in a bedsheet. Music.*)

FERNIE. Yo, Vick.

VICKY. Where are you calling me from?

FERNIE. The office. I'm gonna be home late. Don't wait up for me.

VICKY. What's that I hear in the background?

FERNIE. Fax machine. It's acting up. Love you. Gotta go.

VICKY. Fernando, I got Tommy over here right now and he wants me to –

FERNIE. Great. Why don't you two rent a movie? I gotta go.

(**FERNIE** *begins a long, slow march off.*)

Get your ass ready. Your body's about to know Raza. It's about to drink gold. You gonna plumb the depth of my race and suck the long dick of history. Fuse yourself to the glories of Aztlan. The million gods of invasion are gonna swarm on you and turn your flesh to fire!

And remember, tonight, baby, your name is Victoria!

(*He goes.*)

VICKY. How much do you need?

TOMAS. Ninety K.

VICKY. Are we gonna see any of it back?

(**TOMAS** *looks away.*)

What do I care? It's not my business. I'll get it. But don't leave me alone tonight, Tommy. This night the thing I need most is you.

TOMAS. You're my brother's wife, remember?

(**VICKY** *slams the suitcase shut and stands apart as* **WILLIS, MIKE, PEGGY, FELECIA, GONZALEZ,** *and the* **JUDGE** *enter.* **MIKE** *stands with a deck of bingo cards. During the following sequence,* **PEGGY** *and* **FELECIA** *provide props for the* **JUDGE** *as* **WILLIS** *observes the action with stopwatch and binoculars. The* **JUDGE** *walks to the designated areas to indicate movement within time and space.)*

WILLIS. This is the Day of Whack.

TOMAS. Phase one.

PEGGY. The Judge wakes at 6:00 every morning.

JUDGE. But today, a vivid dream stirs me at 5:57.

TOMAS. The exact time I open my eyes.

PEGGY. He gets up, fetches the paper from the slot in his door.

FELECIA. He showers, dresses, makes breakfast for him and his biddy.

JUDGE. I read my daily passage from the Book of Psalms.

TOMAS. I read mine from the Judges.

WILLIS. And he goes to his car. He uses an automatic garage door opener.

JUDGE. I drive in silence, the faint remembrance of the dream filtering through my mind.

TOMAS. As he drives south, I drive north to Vicky's house for the money.

MIKE. In the jail, Camacho and me wager for our souls in a game of *Loteria.*

GONZALEZ. I prepare the opening statement for the trial.

TOMAS. Phase two.

PEGGY. He goes down Broadway and arrives at the parking garage downtown at 7:45.

FELECIA. And he ain't wearing no bulletproof vest.

JUDGE. On this day a comely young creature is bending over the open hood of her car. The security officers are helping her out.

VICKY. I bring the money in my suitcase and we count it.

PEGGY. He parks in his assigned space and goes through an underway to the Federal Courthouse.

FELECIA. While the cop is with me, Pappy slips inside and goes to his car.

WILLIS. I quietly break in and take the batteries from the garage door opener. Then I replace it, lock the car, and stroll away.

MIKE. *LA CORONA.*

PEGGY. His first case is at 8:00. He comes five minutes early every day, barring weekends and holidays.

WILLIS. He sees both misdemeanor and felony cases all morning long.

JUDGE. There is a faint ringing in my ears during some hearings.

TOMAS. It's the breach. I hear it again getting louder.

GONZALEZ. I am going to win this case.

MIKE. *EL CATRIN.*

TOMAS. Phase three.

FELECIA. At 9:32 I fly out to Midland where I check into a Best Western.

WILLIS. *(As* **PEGGY** *enters with a rifle and ammo.)* And I prepare the hardware Peg bought me three weeks before.

PEGGY. This here's a Mauser 98 Bolt-action Rifle. Mostly used for deer, this baby has a sweet-as-pie adjustable trigger. It's real light, real smooth, and real strong. It's chambered for the 7mmm Magnum cartridge, and I bought me the 100 grain hollow-point. I also picked out a top-of-the-line Leupold 10x Silver scope. With these crosshairs you can shoot the head off a sparrow at three hundred yards.

WILLIS. Peg, you know I would never do that. Birds are sacred.

PEGGY. You know what name I bought it under? Ida B. Lyon.

WILLIS. Damn, I dunno which I like better: my guns or my women.

(**NENA** *comes on to take the suitcase from* **VICKY**.)

TOMAS. Phase four. When we are done counting, Nena comes over and takes the load.

NENA. *Me pongo mis sunglasses* and catch me a plane to Midland.

MIKE. *EL PAJARO.*

GONZALEZ. I am going to bring down Santos & Santos.

FELECIA. I lie in bed in my panties eatin' fajita-pitas and watchin' HBO.

PEGGY. At 11:30 he breaks for lunch to Joseph's Deli, usually in the company of other jurists or big-time city politicos.

JUDGE. I take a chance on the combination Mexican plate.

WILLIS. He has two cocktails with lunch and tips like a woman.

PEGGY. He goes back at 1:00 and resumes his hearing and the like, until 3:00, which is when he's done for the day.

JUDGE. This dream is nagging me on the way to my car. It has bedeviled my whole day.

TOMAS. Phase five. Vicky closes the store early and joins me at her house.

MIKE. *LA MANO.*

GONZALEZ. The only way now is up. I'm going to score.

WILLIS. He drives back Alamo Heights way to the Country Club, where he's a standing member, and suits up for a game of tennis.

PEGGY. He plays hard with any one of a small circle of geezers with overdeveloped calves. Judge definitely likes to win.

JUDGE. But this day I lose when a face from the dream seizes me for a flash and makes me miss the ball. My insides are burning.

TOMAS. Phase six.

FELECIA. At 4:00 I get a call. Then a knock at 4:05.

NENA. *(With the suitcase.)* Where's your father?

FELECIA. Out.

NENA. I'm supposed to leave this with you?

FELECIA. That's my understanding.

NENA. The key's inside.

FELECIA. How'm I supposed to open it?

NENA. You're not.

(**NENA** *drops the suitcase.* **FELECIA** *takes it.*)

PEGGY. I get a call shortly thereafter.

TOMAS. Phase seven.

WILLIS. At 5:30 he showers and phones his wife from the lobby.

PEGGY. By 5:50 he's headed home. Takes a left out of the driveway, goes right, then right again, then left, then straight, then left.

TOMAS. In the evening with all the lights in the house out, we sit in front of a TV neither of us have the nerve to turn on.

MIKE. *EL DIABLITO.*

WILLIS. He pulls into his garage at 6:00 on the nose. A creature of meticulous habit.

JUDGE. The garage won't open. Push the pad again and wait.

TOMAS. We wait.

PEGGY. The second he pushes the garage door opener, I'm packing our stuff into the car.

FELECIA. I'm over Ft. Worth on Southwest Fl. 401.

WILLIS. I'm on the roof of the Victory Arms Apartment Complex aiming the Model 98 Mauser rifle with the high power telescopic sight across eight clean manicured suburban lawns.

JUDGE. The garage won't open. Then in a great fit of gas, it occurs to me. The entire dream.

WILLIS. He gets out of his car. An abstract look on his face that I really hate to mess up.

PEGGY/FELECIA . He walks to his front door.

GONZALEZ. Then I hear it on the news.

MIKE/NENA/VICKY. *EL CORAZON.*

TOMAS. Now.

JUDGE. The dream. The middle of this narrow street, cobbled with greasy stones that shine like exposed ulcers in the green light of the streetlamp. Overhead the night opens its mouth to me with a sound like steam. Old crumbling buildings with the shutters drawn. No one out. One doorway has a sheet draped over it. I peer inside. There, on a stinking mattress, lit by a candle, Paloma. Her knees drawn up to her chin, her black hair falling over her face. She's young all over again. With a look, she draws me to her and we are in each others' arms, kissing and groping under worn sheets. I am aware only of her muffled cries, but when I finally come, I feel something like a single burning heartbeat shoot through my spine, shoot, shoot right through, and it comes out the small of my back and I am suspended in air. Then I look up beside me, and standing over me, I see him. I see him with the eyes of judgment pressing into me.

TOMAS. What time is it?

VICKY. I don't know.

TOMAS. Don't turn the light on.

VICKY. What's happened?

FELECIA. The phone rings.

TOMAS. Final phase. Yes.

WILLIS. To-weee. To-weee.

TOMAS. Is it done?

WILLIS. I rang his bell. Once for you.

> (**WILLIS** *fires his rifle. A tremendous crack. The* **JUDGE** *falls to the floor with a cry.*)

And once for me.

(He fires again. The **JUDGE** *groans and is still.)*

WILLIS. *(Cont.)* It was a pleasure to serve you.

MIKE. *La muerte.*

(Everyone goes, but **VICKY**, **TOMAS**, *and the* **JUDGE**.*)*

VICKY. Who was it?

TOMAS. Judge Benton is dead.

VICKY. Is this...what I paid for?

(He starts to take his clothes off.)

TOMAS. These are the wages of brotherhood.

VICKY. Tommy...have you...murdered this man?

TOMAS. *(Moving toward her half-undressed.)* These are the wounds that bind us.

VICKY. TOMMY!

TOMAS. Our blood is now blood of the house.

VICKY. WHAT DID YOU MAKE ME DO! DEAR GOD IN HEAVEN!

TOMAS. *(Taking her in his arms.)* Now we are fully made. Familia, Santos.

(Black out. She cries in the darkness.)

End of Act II

ACT III

*(**GONZALEZ** at the press conference. Flashing bulbs of cameras.)*

GONZALEZ. This is a grievous day. The brutal slaying of this fair-minded man who devoted his life to the Texas Court, cut down like a dog in his own front yard, is a crime which deepens our shame. But mark my words: from this shame I draw fire. I will not rest until the person or persons responsible for this outrage are apprehended, tried, and convicted.

(He steps glumly out of the light, pauses, then unleashes a grito of jubilation.)

AAAAAAAAAAA-HOOOOOOOOOOOOOOOOOO-AAAAAAAAAAAA!

*(**NENA**, more visibly pregnant, enters.)*

NENA. What are you so happy about?

GONZALEZ. If you had anything to do with this killing, lady, God bless you. Your family has just clinched my fame!

NENA. What are you talking about? The Judge is dead.

GONZALEZ. Between us, *señora*, I hated the man. Crusty old fart was a bully, a bigot, and he never remembered my name. But now, without lifting a finger, I've moved from a routine narcotics probe to the crime of the decade. That's what I call upward mobility!

NENA. You talk like you're the one who shot the Judge.

GONZALEZ. *(Producing a set of tapes.)* Not me, *señora*, but as Benton's grieving avenger, I should warn you: one word of murder in these Santos sessions, and I'm gonna try you, dry you, and fry you till you're black as beans. God, I love this country!

(He goes. **NENA** *turns to the table where* **MIKE**, *haggard and weak, waits.)*

NENA. To hell with him and his stupid tapes. The new judge has a lenient face.

Tommy ain't been seen much. Vicky's the last one he talked to. *Que bueno que hicieron* postpone el trial. Fernie needs the time.

Viejo, remember that whole mess of cash from Santos Furniture we used? We couldn't pay it back. The bank took over the business. After thirty years in this dumb town. When Fernando found out about it, he hit the roof. And then the *pendejo* hit his wife.

*(*FERNIE *drags* VICKY *in, her face swollen and bleeding.)*

FERNIE. What the fuck were you thinking? That store's been in our family for years!

VICKY. Let me go!

FERNIE. We entrusted you with that business. My old man signed it over to you. How could you do this? What did you do with the money?

VICKY. I gave it away to charity, just like you big boys.

FERNIE. Don't fuck with me Vicky! I'll knock your teeth across the room!

VICKY. All right! All right! Let me go.

FERNIE. *Orale.* Level with me. Where's the money?

VICKY. In the judge.

FERNIE. Say what?

VICKY. Half went through his heart. The other half through his spinal column.

NENA. She told him everything, but it didn't do her no good.

*(*FERNIE *drags her out as she screams for help.)*

He beat the hell out of her, *Viejo.* The thing was she was pregnant, and she lost the baby. Your brother he killed his own kid. *Lastima.* That woman used to be the pride of the Lower Valley. Otherwise, things are back to normal. I bought the girls some new clothes for school and the baby's room's almost done.

(**MIKE** *nods slowly and rises.*)

MIKE. Nena, all these months in this shithole have made me see things clearly. You know what we need to do as a *raza*? We need to learn to ski. That's right. And play a lotta polo! We gotta drink bottled water and eat bland foods. Fuck, we gotta learn to speak English.

NENA. We do.

MIKE. Yeah, but not as good as the Muppets. We gotta think different, we gotta think mini-series! I see it so clearly. Jail is just the thing we Mexicans need!

(**MIKE** *charges off.* **NENA** *crosses herself as* **VICKY** *enters, shaking with rage.* **FERNIE** *enters separately.*)

FERNIE. Vicky. I know what's what.

VICKY. What are you talking about?

FERNIE. That kid wasn't mine. We haven't slept together in months.

VICKY. What do you want, a prize?

FERNIE. Whose was it?

VICKY. Get off my case, Negro. You never told me about your little flings!

FERNIE. Whose kid was it!

VICKY. First you tell me who you've been seeing on the side.

FERNIE. Are you listening to that talk again? Who's been feeding you this line?

(**PAM** *emerges from the other side.*)

PAM. Me.

FERNIE. You told her?

PAM. What was I supposed to do? She looked at me with those swollen eyes and asked for the truth. I told her the truth.

VICKY. Everything.

FERNIE. *Orale,* Vicky, this ain't so bad. We'll see a counselor.

VICKY. You see a counselor. I'm seeing a lawyer.

PAM. Man who does that to his wife, I want no part of it.

FERNIE. Shut up! You're fired!

PAM. *(Throwing her balled up resignation in his face.)* Too late! I'm gone! Write your own memos, counselor.

     *(**PAM** goes. **TOMAS** enters and watches.)*

VICKY. Get out of my house.

FERNIE. *Orale,* Vicky –

VICKY. GET OUT OF MY HOUSE!

     *(**FERNIE** goes. **VICKY** sits and holds herself steady.)*

TOMAS. [*Mi carnal.* The Aztec god of bullshit. Four hundred years of degenerate blood. His own kid on the altar. Offered up to America. The miscarriage of justice.]

VICKY. About time you showed up. Where have you been hiding? You missed the show.

TOMAS. There were some things I had to clear up.

VICKY. Do you know about my miscarriage?

TOMAS. Yes, I was – god, what did he do to you?

VICKY. Don't, Tommy. Please don't look at me like that. It doesn't help.

TOMAS. Shithead.

VICKY. Quit it, Tommy. I'm over it.

TOMAS. How could he do this to you!

VICKY. I'm leaving him.

TOMAS. Where are you going?

VICKY. Away from here. I don't have to live in a house of someone else's effects. I want my own furniture. As far as I'm concerned, this is the year one and you are all gone.

TOMAS. You can't leave now, Vick.

VICKY. Just watch me.

TOMAS. What about the family?

VICKY. You're the family now. You've taken the Santos name to new lows.

TOMAS. What about us? We started something. You walk out on me and everything blacks out.

VICKY. At one point…in the kitchen… I was curled up against the trash compactor as Negro kicked the shit out of me…and I started to black out. My body started to fill with this thick liquid and a calm that I have never felt before swept me out of my pain. With all my being I invited death. I wanted to close my eyes and die. I wanted not to be this woman, this hurt not to hurt, and my blood not to bleed on the linoleum. But then this scream rose from my womb and tore through my lungs.

(In the faintest whisper.)

Tommy –

Negro just looked at me. Couldn't do nothing else but look.

TOMAS. You leave him to me. I'll fix him.

VICKY. I wouldn't blame Fernie too much. It wasn't his baby. It was yours.

(The **JUDGE** *enters.)*

TOMAS. Mine?

JUDGE. Your son. Flesh of your flesh.

VICKY. You got death on you like a frost, Tommy.

JUDGE. Corpus delicti.

VICKY. So long. I don't want any of you glorious Santos fucks coming near me ever again.

(She goes.)

TOMAS. [My son.

JUDGE. Conceived on the day of my slaughter.

TOMAS. No. It couldn't be mine. I wouldn't let my baby… I would have taken care.

JUDGE. Denial. Trait of a nation with its roots in treason. Michael screws his community, you screw him, he screws the biker, and you screw the whole kitnkaboodle. Cycles of betrayal.

TOMAS. Right after the shooting, I went across the border to J-town. La Mariscal. I drowned myself in whores and tequila in celebration of your death. On my last night, they brought in the dregs. A withered stalk of an old whore, with painted eyes and the yellow teeth of a monkey. Dressed in the tattered bathrobe of an old john. She told me her name in this cigarette voice as she slipped her bones over my leg. That's when I knew. This was your symbol, the one you cherished. Your Paloma.

JUDGE. My symbol never ages. She just moves on to the next one. From my arm…

> (*Showing him his forearm, where the tattoo has disappeared.*)

…to yours.

> (**TOMAS** *rolls back his sleeve, discovering the tattoo of the bleeding heart on his arm. The* **JUDGE** *goes.*)

TOMAS. Branded on me forever the sign of Mexican descent the heart taken from its vault sense severed from sense la vida worth a few centavos forever on me now.]

> (**WILLIS** *enters, gazing at the sky. The sound of surf.*)

WILLIS. I like coming to the beach. There's a great variety of sea birds along the Gulf coast. Gulls, terns, bitterns, sandpipers. They know where the feeding is… Where you get the tattoo, kid?

TOMAS. In Juarez. Do you have it?

WILLIS. *(Producing a small paper bag.)* Indeed I do. You ever pop one of these?

TOMAS. No.

WILLIS. Basic handgun. Won't go off unless you fire it. You sure this ain't a job for me?

TOMAS. *(Taking the gun out of the bag.)* No. This is an affair I take care of myself.

WILLIS. *(As he hands him the ammo.)* I'm entitled to know who you're whackin', kid.

TOMAS. *(Loading the gun.)* It's a family matter.

WILLIS. You ever done one, Tomboy? It's a high. Very few vocations confront you with the Great Void, if you see my meaning. For a second, you're right on the cusp of a great tension between the powers of life and death. You can almost see the bare tissue stretchin' in the air before you, like a muscle. And then bam, it's over.

TOMAS. I know what it's like.

WILLIS. You only think you do.

TOMAS. *(Aiming the gun squarely at him.)* Okay, wiseass, tell us about dying. Or don't you know what this end of the gun is like?

WILLIS. Hey now.

> *(**TOMAS** produces from his packets **CAMACHO**'s teeth.)*

TOMAS. Open wide. AAAAAAHHH!

> *(**WILLIS** opens wide. **TOMAS** crams the teeth in his mouth. **WILLIS** gurgles.)*

Remember these? They're Camacho's. The teeth of a man with no cause to die.

> *(**WILLIS** gags and spits them out.)*

You may pull the trigger, Casper, but I will it. I live it down. That's the power a cheap gun-for-hire like you will never understand. I assume responsibility. I assume the guilt. There's power in that.

WILLIS. I reckon there is.

(**TOMAS** *turns away. The hammering sound.*)

TOMAS. Hear it? The breach. I got the doom beating on me like a drum.

Bu-bum bu-bum bu-bum.

WILLIS. Bottle it up, boy. You don't want to vent that. I suggest you get yourself a hobby. Like rare coins, or fossils. Or birds.

(**TOMAS** *goes.* **WILLIS** *dusts himself off and turns to* **PEGGY** *and* **FELECIA** *reveling over the open suitcase overflowing with dollar bills.*)

FELECIA. WOOOOOeeee! Money money money money money!

PEGGY. It sure is pretty, Casper.

WILLIS. Reap and ye shall sow, saith the Lord.

FELECIA. Does this mean we can get cable?

WILLIS. Sure does, baby. (*To* **PEGGY**.) What'd you do with the rifle?

PEGGY. It's gatherin' fish shit in Lake Ray Hubbard.

FELECIA. Can I have my cut in hundred dollar bill denominations, Pappy?

WILLIS. Not just yet. We're stashin' it away for the time bein'. Peg, you put this in our shed. I'm drivin' to Lubbock and El Paso to invest the rest. Send a check to the Audubon Society while you're at it.

FELECIA. Bye, Pappy. Give me a kissy-hug.

(*He drops a handful of bills down her shorts and goes.*)

Lookit what he gave me! Five hundred smackers!

PEGGY. Give it here.

FELECIA. Uh-uh! These are mine.

PEGGY. Felecia Lee, you're not spendin' any of it till things settle down. Now, you let me put that –

FELECIA. NO! I'm goin' to Neiman's and buyin' me a new dress and some new flats with this.

PEGGY. You're doin' no such a thing. Give it!

FELECIA. What, and let you blow it on another bad hairdo? No way Jose.

PEGGY. For your information, that's part of our vacation fund. We're going on a Caribbean cruise.

FELECIA. I don't want to go on no cruise.

PEGGY. Who said you were? You're going to school, missy, and learning you some manners. Casper and me are going by ourselves.

FELECIA. Fat chance. Pappy's not going anywhere without me.

PEGGY. What makes you say that?

FELECIA. He's just not, least of all on some boring old boat with you.

PEGGY. You have got a liberal mouth on you, girl.

FELECIA. He loves me in a deep and everlastin' way.

PEGGY. Pipe dreams.

FELECIA. Ain't no pipe dream he's pokin' me with, Momma.

PEGGY. Come again?

FELECIA. You might as well know. We're in love.

PEGGY. What the hell are you saying?

FELECIA. We're lovers. Been so for six months now.

PEGGY. You're lying.

FELECIA. We done it every time you been out. He even told me, the best part about being with you was being with me. We're lovers. You got no choice in the matter.

PEGGY. I reckon I don't.

> *(Pause. Then* **PEGGY** *calmly rises and goes to the phone.)*

Hello, FBI, please.

FELECIA. What are you doing!

PEGGY. Any extension will do, thank you.

FELECIA. *(Rushing up and snatching the phone from her.)* Stop it! Hang up!

PEGGY. I want to report –

FELECIA. Momma! No! No! Hang up! Hang it!

PEGGY. Hold on. There seems to be some interference…

> *(They fight for the phone. **PEGGY** finally slaps **FELECIA** down. She retrieves the receiver as **FELECIA** cries.)*

Now. Let's have us a little talk about this judge.

> *(**GONZALEZ** marches in as **PEGGY** drags **FELECIA** off. He stands with the tape recorder. The following sequence represents taped telephone exchanges involving **TOMAS**, **VICKY**, **NENA**, **FERNIE**, and **WILLIS**. They speak in rapid agitated tones.)*

VICKY. Answer the phone, dammit. Answer the phone. Answer it.

NENA. Diga.

VICKY. Nena!

NENA. What?

VICKY. You alone?

NENA. Yeah.

VICKY. Nena, the Feds know.

NENA. Fuck.

VICKY. You gotta split to Mexico, man. Go.

NENA. I'll deal with it.

VICKY. Go! Get your kids and your ass to J-town, NOW!

NENA. I'm not going. I'm not going back to Mexico. I'm not a Mexican!

VICKY. Nena!

TOMAS. Vicky!

VICKY. What!

TOMAS. I just got the word that –

VICKY. I know already! I know!

TOMAS. Deny everything! Deny it!

VICKY. What are you gonna do!

TOMAS. Later! Call Nena!

VICKY. I did already!

TOMAS. Call Fernie.

FERNIE. Vicky!

VICKY. That's him on the other line!

TOMAS. Bye!

VICKY. Fernie, it's me.

FERNIE. *Malas noticias,* Vick.

VICKY. I know, I know.

FERNIE. Shit meets fan. Fan turns. Shit flies. End of story.

VICKY. What are we gonna do?

FERNIE. Honey, your problem. I didn't have squat to do with this.

VICKY. Then clear off the line. Nena!

NENA. No. I'm not going anywhere.

VICKY. There isn't time to argue, Nena!

NENA. Someone's on the other line.

TOMAS. Nena!

NENA. *Olvidalo, Tomas.* I'm staying right here with Michael.

TOMAS. Hold on, I got another call.

WILLIS. We're in trouble, kid.

TOMAS. Your wife is a rat, Casper. Where are you?

WILLIS. Not staying. I recommend the open road.

TOMAS. I don't know you.

WILLIS. I don't know you.

TOMAS. Get off the line! Nena!

GONZALEZ. Hello, Tommy.

> (*A pause.* **TOMAS** *is distressed at this new voice.*)

Hello.

> (**TOMAS** *slowly backs away.*)

NENA. Tomas, answer the phone.

FERNIE. *De volada,* bro. Answer.

NENA. I know you're there, Tomas.

VICKY. Answer, dammit. Answer the phone.

*(All disperse except **NENA** who turns on a vacuum cleaner and **VICKY** who goes to **MIKE**, **CAMACHO** standing by him. They sit still a moment. The vacuum goes off.)*

VICKY.
It was awful, Mike.
She was cleaning 'cause the maid had quit a week before.
That's when they came for her.
There were cops everywhere, all
Over the house, but it was
Gonzalez who came in to serve her.

That Willis woman fingered her along with Tommy.

*(**NENA** looks down at the vacuum in bewilderment.)*
(She flips the switch to make it come on again, to no avail.)

*(She turns around to see **GONZALEZ** walking in.)*

*(**GONZALEZ** produces a document which he hands to her.)*

*(**NENA** scans the document in silence.)*

VICKY.
All he said was…

and touched her elbow, when she cut loose.

GONZALEZ.
I thought you should know. I come from La Colonia too.

(With a cry, she raises the stem of the vacuum cleaner over her head and swings it at him, striking him hard. She struggles to get away, but he chases after her, grabbing her by the legs. She collapses, kicking and swinging her fists at him.)

But then something
happened.

    *(**NENA** hunches over in great pain as **GONZALEZ**
    holds her down.)*

VICKY. It took hours, a shitload of doctors, and a *rosario*
at Nena's house, but he came through fine. The baby
came through fine.

MIKE. This is our ascension! *(Standing.)* To be born at the
precious moment of his mother's arrest! The child is
vindication!

    *(Going to **NENA** and **GONZALEZ** who are still on
    the floor.)*

WATCH THIS BABY! THIS BABY MUST BE NURSED
ON PURE HOMOGENOUS MILK! *NO CHILE, NO
PAN DULCE*, NOT A SINGLE PINTO BEAN! IF HE
IS TO BE A TRUE AMERICAN HE MUST LIVE, HE
MUST CATCH THE DISCO FEVER, HE MUST SET
HIS BROS AFIRE!

    (He reaches in his pocket and produces a match.)

I'll light a *vela* for him.

    (He charges off.)

VICKY. Yeah. Nena's okay, too.

    *(**TOMAS** enters carrying the painting of Zapata, as
    VICKY, **NENA** and **GONZALEZ** recede.)*

TOMAS. [Tomas Santos, revised bilingual edition. First
generation. Born in el pisso del norte. Ex-tex-mex.

    *(Placing it on the table, he scrapes off the cocaine
    with a letter opener and rubs it against his gums.
    DON MIGUEL appears.)*

DON MIGUEL. *Tomas Tomas Tomas*. Finally my youngest
leaves for his American life.

TOMAS. *Papa*, I don't know what to do. Everything leads to
death.

DON MIGUEL. I finished just in time for you to see. This one I made special just for me. See how Concordia erupts from the wood?

TOMAS. *Tenemos nada.* This world is nothing. People are as thin as lies.

DON MIGUEL. Before you go, *hazme un favor, mijo.* The only thing I ask of you.

TOMAS. Anything.

DON MIGUEL. Promise to betray me. When the time comes, promise to turn against your father. It is what anyone who wants to succeed in this land must do. I did it to *mis padres* and your children will do it to you. But in the end, remember this. You are the first law.

TOMAS. The first law.

DON MIGUEL. *Mira,* my finest piece. I'll be buried in it like a king.

FERNIE. *(Offstage.)* TOMMY! YO!

DON MIGUEL. *(As he fades.) Dios te bendiga, hijo mio.]*

(**FERNIE** *enters.*)

FERNIE. Where the hell you been, man? Everybody's been lookin' for you.

TOMAS. I know.

FERNIE. What are you doin' here?

TOMAS. Look, Negro. The whole place dusted for prints and they missed Zapata.

FERNIE. C'mon, bro. Let me get you out of here.

TOMAS. Did they get the others?

FERNIE. All except you.

TOMAS. Even ol' Casper?

FERNIE. Hell yeah. He was easy.

(**WILLIS** *staggers in, shirtless and in shorts, carrying a gym bag and a loaded gun.*)

He was goin' ninety on Interstate 10 in his T-bird with a shitload of cash and cocaine. *Vato estaba todo* paranoid.

WILLIS. How could I not be paranoid? My own women betrayed me. They revealed me to the Law and brought ruin on my head.

FERNIE. He was so coked up that when his muffler started backfiring, he thought the Feds had put a tracer on him.

WILLIS. They bugged my car! I had no choice but to pull over in the middle of the desert and get out my gun and stand over my T. I said Kyrie Eleison over the shiny red hood and Bam! Bam! Bam! Bam! Bam! Bam! I sent the ol' girl on like a lame horse.

FERNIE. He ruined a perfectly good car.

WILLIS. I wiped a dusty tear, reloaded my gun and then my nose, and started walking east on I-One-Oh.

TOMAS. What a maniac.

FERNIE. He's waving a gun in hundred degree heat in the middle of Bumfuck, Texas, trying to flag down passing cars, when who comes along?

WILLIS. The posse!

FERNIE. El Highway Patrol. Soon four cars are circled around this *gringo* lunatic with a gun and a gym bag full of cash.

TOMAS. So what did they do?

WILLIS. *(Putting the gun under his chin.)* Don't come any closer! I'll put a blowhole through my head! No-one's taking me alive!

FERNIE. Fool started ranting all sortsa shit.

WILLIS. On behalf of my avian brothers, I bequeath my body to the open air where the birds may pick my bones clean! I shall be part and parcel of the fowls above! Kreee! Kreee!

TOMAS. I don't believe it.

FERNIE. Bull all of five minutes later.

WILLIS. *(Throwing his hands up.)* Aw, forget this. It's just too damn hot. Any y'all gotta Big Red Soda Pop?

TOMAS. Did he confess?

FERNIE. Oh yeah.

WILLIS. Hey now, I never touched the judge, but I confess unto God, I'm the Grassy Knoll. I popped Jack Kennedy. I popped Marilyn too. And JR Ewing too! Pit-a-zee! Pit-a-zee!

(He exits.)

FERNIE. You're the only one left. You been bad, *ese*. The community is like major disappointed in you.

TOMAS. I bet they are.

FERNIE. What the hell are you doing here?

TOMAS. I'm mourning the death of my child.

FERNIE. Say what?

TOMAS. The breach has rattled its little bones to mush. And I come to mourn.

(They gaze at each other. Crossfade to **GONZALEZ** *in full light. Press conference.)*

GONZALEZ. In the spiraling events since the tragic slaying of Judge Benton, our office – in conjunction with the FBI – has spent millions of dollars and thousands of man-hours conducting its most thorough probe in history. I'm announcing today the arrest of several suspects allegedly involved in the assassination. These include:

(Formally parading his suspects.)

Casper Thomas Willis, professional hitman.

*(***WILLIS** *trots by waving his handcuffs to the cameras.)*

His wife Peggy Tomlinson.

*(***PEGGY** *rushes past with her face hidden.)*

Her daughter who is a minor.

*(***FELECIA,** *distraught and weeping, goes by.)*

Michael Santos who is in custody and awaiting trial on drug racketeering charges.

MIKE. *¡Mexicanos! ¡Pochos!* Hear what I say! Give up your *Virgen,* go Scientology and listen to the Beach Boys! Dye your hair blonde and sin no more! *¡DISNEYLANDIA!*

GONZALEZ. His wife Magdalena Ruiz Santos

(**NENA** *is quickly conveyed in a wheelchair.*)

Pamela Hanson, who works for the Law Office of Santon & Santos.

(**PAM** *strides by like a model wearing sunglasses.*)

And Tomas Santos, considered by our office to be the mastermind.

(**TOMAS** *crosses by, betraying no expression.*)

He is also charged with first-degree murder in the shooting death of his brother Fernando, who was found dead in their law office. We're questioning other possible accomplices to the assassination.

(**VICKY** *appears.*)

VICKY. No.

GONZALEZ. Let me rephrase the question: Did you help kill the judge?

VICKY. I'll rephrase my answer: Fuck no.

GONZALEZ. Tommy asked you for the money.

VICKY. He didn't tell me what for.

GONZALEZ. It was shipped in your suitcase.

VICKY. Which I'd given Tommy two weeks before.

GONZALEZ. You and Tommy seem to be pretty intimate.

VICKY. What is this shit? Just because you're the man of the hour, you think you can say whatever you want to my face? Excuse me, Batman, I've got a husband to bury.

(*She gets up.*)

GONZALEZ. Sit down. I said, SIT DOWN.

(**VICKY** *sits.*)

Don't try your Rottweiler act with me 'cause I will meet you halfway, *ruca.* I'll charge you with withholding evidence and put you away for YEARS. Since this case started, I've been shunned, slandered, and called a *vendido*. My family has received death threats. But that's business. I know what I am, and I know what I sacrificed to be what I am. I live the life I want. I just want to know what motive Tomas would have for shooting your husband.

VICKY. Tommy loved his brothers. He'd never sacrifice them for a career.

GONZALEZ. Have you ever seen this man?

> (**WILLIS**, *in prison greys, and* **FELECIA** *at the table.*)

WILLIS. Lesha doll.

FELECIA. They let me out, Pappy.

WILLIS. That's good.

FELECIA. They said they didn't have enough on me. The lawyer said he might could get me off if I testify against you.

WILLIS. Well, you know better than that, don't you?

FELECIA. Uh-huh. I'm so mad at her, Pappy. I can't believe she turned us in.

WILLIS. Your momma has a mean streak.

FELECIA. It just riles me. She did it to keep us apart, you know.

WILLIS. Yahweh will punish her.

FELECIA. They said, when they caught you, that you were driving back to Dallas to kill us both.

WILLIS. I wouldn't do a nasty thing like that, would I?

FELECIA. I s'ppose. Oh, Pappy, I miss you. All 'cause of that judge. You should'na killed him.

WILLIS. I didn't, honey pie.

FELECIA. You didn't?

WILLIS. Well, I admit I shed his grace all over his front yard, but until they find the rifle, they have the wrong man. Now, why'nt you slung over and let me feel the sweetness of you for Pappy's sake?

FELECIA. Here? We can't do it here.

WILLIS. Nobody's watching. Slung over and lemme dip my chip.

FELECIA. Later, Pappy. When you get out.

WILLIS. That may be a while. Felecia Lee, don't vex me. Lean in.

> (**FELECIA** *slumps in her seat toward* **WILLIS.** *He slips his hand under the table between her legs.*)

Oh, honey. I been missing you so bad. I feel like bustin' wide open with –

> (**WILLIS** *withdraws his hand, producing a small button with a long thin cord attached from under her dress.*)

The hell is this?

> (**GONZALEZ** *steps forward with the tape player.*)

FELECIA. Sorry, Pappy.

> (**GONZALEZ** *plays it.* **WILLIS**' *voice broadcasts loudly over speakers:* "Well, I admit I shed his grace all over his front yard, but until they find the rifle, they have the wrong man.")

WILLIS. You? You wearin' a wire?

> (**FELECIA** *quickly retracts her bug and scrambles away.* **WILLIS** *pounds the table like a madman.*)

YOU LITTLE BITCH! YOU GOT A WIRE! DAMN YOU! YOU TREASONOUS LITTLE TART! YOU DONE HANGED ME BY A WIRE! YOU HEAR! YOU HANGED ME! GOD! THESE WIRES! THESE GODDAMN WIRES! HELL WILL BE A PLACE OF WIRES!

> (*He stomps off, tearing off the buttons from his shirt and ranting to himself.* **GONZALEZ** *turns to* **VICKY.**)

VICKY. No. I've never seen him.

GONZALEZ. You're free to go, Mrs. Santos…for now.

> *(He goes.* **VICKY** *puts on her veil and slowly crosses the stage toward* **TOMAS**.*)*

VICKY. *Cordero de Dios, que quitas el pecado del mundo,*
Ten piedad de nosotros.
Cordero de Dios, que quitas el pecado del mundo,
Ten piedad de nosotros.
Cordero de Dios, que quitas el pecado del mundo,
Danos la paz.

> *(She joins him at the table.)*

VICKY. Fernie was buried this morning.

TOMAS. *Dios ten piedad.*

VICKY. I was only one at the graveside. Everyone else is in jail.

TOMAS. How's Mike?

VICKY. He's up for the chair. Nena just wants her shoes.

TOMAS. The baby's okay?

VICKY. He's fine. He comes into my custody tomorrow.

TOMAS. What about the Willises?

VICKY. All but the daughter are getting charged. She's the star witness. Everybody's testifying against each other. Except you. Nobody wants to sell you out.

TOMAS. It's good to see you, Vicky. Even in your weeds.

VICKY. I thought all my feeling for Fernando was gone. But right when they started to lower him into the ground, out of nowhere, these tears came spilling down my face. I couldn't make them stop. I cried all the way home for a worm who treated me nice only as an afterthought. The heart just never gives up, does it?

TOMAS. That's what makes it a heart.

VICKY. What happened with you and Fernie, Tomas?

TOMAS. There is no point in trying to –

VICKY. You haven't told me. I want to know. Did you kill my husband?

(**TOMAS** *looks toward the conference table for a moment.*)

TOMAS. I came to mourn the death of my child.

(**FERNIE** *comes out of the shadows.*)

FERNIE. Say what?

(**TOMAS** *rises and joins him.* **VICKY** *watches.*)

TOMAS. The breach has rattled its little bones to mush.

FERNIE. Are you tripping?

TOMAS. *Carnal,* I am gonna level with you. The child Vicky lost wasn't yours. It was mine. My baby.

FERNIE. What are you talking about?

TOMAS. That was my baby you beat outa her.

FERNIE. You…and my wife?

TOMAS. That ain't the half of it. If you knew the shit I been up to.

FERNIE. Then fuckin' tell me.

TOMAS. That bust at Gila Stables, I made that call. I'm the nark. I got Camacho killed, put Mikey in jail and ruined his family. I had the Judge killed with money from Dad's store, and then I boned your wife and caused my own kid to die.

(*He produces the gun.*)

Soy traicionero, Negro.

(*Slowly advancing on* **FERNIE** *with the gun.*)

Santos & Santos. Sons of La Malinche. *Hijos de la chingada madre.* Poor bitch. I know how she feels.

(*He puts the gun in* **FERNIE**'s *hand.*)

Orale. Whenever you're ready.

(**FERNIE** *aims the gun at* **TOMAS**, *then drops it.*)

FERNIE. You're my brother.

TOMAS. Negro, you have to do this.

FERNIE. Wise up, *ese.* This is what they want you to do. They want you to rise above the family, to think above the family, NOTHING is above the family. We die without it. Our father left Concordia to carve a new life for himself and his family. And he made it, *ese,* he got his bitchin' American house, but he couldn't have done it without the guts of Aztlan. I'm talkin' heart. The heart knows what borders are crossed. It knows sacrifice. Am I right?

TOMAS. You're right.

FERNIE. We are good people. If we fuck up, it's 'cause we're fuckups. Like anyone else. But you are the only law, the real law, you, *carnal.* Here. You take the damn gun.

(He places it in **TOMAS**' *hand.)*

Aim the thing at my head. Aim it.

*(***TOMAS** *aims it.)*

Can you shoot your brother in the head? That's what you asked me to do. Check out this profile, man. Aztec fucking nose. Dark indio tone. The hair. The thick tongue of my people. We're beautiful, *ese. Chingones.*

VICKY. No, Tommy.

*(***MIKE** *comes out, dressed as he was in the beginning.)*

MIKE. Are you capable of that betrayal?

TOMAS. I don't know.

FERNIE. So?

MIKE. You're gonna be the most famous one of us.

FERNIE. Gonna shoot or not?

MIKE. Your good makes us shine.

TOMAS. We're bastards.

FERNIE. We are princes.

TOMAS. Mongrels.

MIKE. Sons of Gods.

TOMAS. Alone.

MIKE. Never alone.

TOMAS. False.

FERNIE. True as our mother's heart.

VICKY. Don't do it.

TOMAS. I feel the breach.

MIKE. Do you?

VICKY. Tommy…

FERNIE. Do you, brother?

> (**TOMAS** *keeps the gun aimed at his head.*)

TOMAS. [Oh Victoria I aim this 45 caliber guilt right into the face of my bro until I see on my arm the sign the holy sign our justice greater than us tattooed with GRACE I aim at my bro the kind of grace that forgives us all forever forgives us for America forgives us for the blood that runs that will always run I aim grace at my *carnal* Victoria.]

FERNIE. *(Grinning.)* You see? It's not gonna happen. It is not gonna happen.

> (*They remain in this tableau as the lights fade out.*)
>
> *Curtain.*

End of Play